PITCHING

PITCHING

by Dan Schlossberg

Little Simon / Published by Simon & Schuster

NEW YORK / LONDON / TORONTO / SYDNEY / TOKYO / SINGAPORE

A BASEBALL INK BOOK

The views expressed in this book are solely
those of the author and do not necessarily represent
those of Major League Baseball®.

The Major League Baseball® trademarks are used
with the permission of Major League Baseball Properties, Inc.

Photo credits appear on page 85.

LITTLE SIMON
Simon & Schuster Building
Rockefeller Center
1230 Avenue of the Americas
New York, NY 10020

Also available in a SIMON & SCHUSTER BOOKS FOR YOUNG READERS
hardcover edition.

Manufactured in the United States of America
1 3 5 7 9 10 8 6 4 2

Library of Congress Cataloging-in-Publication Data

Schlossberg, Dan, 1948-
Pitching / by Dan Schlossberg
(An Official major league baseball® book)
Summary: Teaches young baseball players how to improve their pitching skills.
1. Pitching (Baseball) — Juvenile literature. [1. Pitching (Baseball)
2. Baseball.] I. Title. II. Series.
GV871.S34   1991 796.357'22 — dc20 90-42099
ISBN 0-671-73317-6
ISBN 0-671-70443-5 (pbk)

To my wife Phyllis, whose love, loyalty, and support

through trying times helped make this book possible

PREFACE

Although numerous pitching instructionals have been published in the past, few have been addressed directly to the Little Leaguer. Some of the existing books contradict each other, others are difficult to understand, and still others are vague on key points. The purpose of this book is therefore both instructional and educational.

This is not a only a how-to book but also a book of advice, hints, and examples. It is aimed at the young pitcher with a real interest in the sport and a dream of advancing as far as his talent and desire will take him. It is also aimed at the fan who wants to know how the best pitchers in the game mastered all of the basics of their complex craft.

Instructions and illustrations in this book alternate between lefthanded and righthanded models; if you are a lefty and the text or photo addresses a righty, simply reverse the terms of the example, substituting right for left or vice versa. And while the male pronoun is used throughout the book just to keep things uncluttered and consistent, all the advice and instruction here apply equally well to girls.

Before he was sidelined by rotator cuff problems in 1990, former Cy Young Award winner Orel Hershiser divided pitching into four major areas: attitude, mechanics, strategy, and regimen. This book covers those four areas and provides the thoughts of many pitchers active in the 1980s and '90s, Hall of Fame hurlers, catchers, managers, and coaches on the art and science of pitching. (The advice of current pitchers will be found in the section called "What the Pitchers Say"; tips from the others, who form this book's panel of coaches, are in "What the Coaches Say.")

We begin with the basics that a young pitcher needs: getting started, practicing patience, and learning the strike zone. Passing each hurdle represents significant progress.

The road to the majors is a difficult one, and very few young pitchers will stay on it to the end. But for those who pursue the dream and work hard to become the best they can be, there are many rewards along the way.

The *Major League Baseball Manual* produced and used by the Milwaukee Brewers provides these guidelines for pitchers:

"The greatest asset a pitcher can have is command: command of himself and command of his pitches.

"To be a consistent winner, a pitcher must (1) have good control—get the first pitch over for a strike; (2) know how to field his position; (3) analyze the hitters—strengths and weaknesses; (4) have confidence; (5) keep his body active—especially the legs. Also, (6) form good pitching habits; (7) concentrate—pick out a spot and throw to it; (8) communicate with his catcher—understand each other; (9) pitch a ball game—don't just be a thrower; (10) back up all bases; (11) be sure to cover first base; and (12) THINK."

These guidelines, prepared for professionals, also apply to the young pitcher participating in his first organized league. A solid foundation for later success can be built by developing the proper physical and mental approach early.

The 300 active major leaguers who started their baseball careers in Little League began building that foundation when they were boys. Many future major leaguers are playing Little League or Babe Ruth or American Legion ball now.

This book is for them, for their parents and coaches, and for baseball fans everywhere.

Dan Schlossberg
Fair Lawn, N.J.

ACKNOWLEDGMENTS

The author is grateful to the many baseball personalities whose generous cooperation was instrumental in the preparation of this book.

In addition to Baseball Ink editors John Thorn and Richard Puff, who provided considerable basic research material, the following individuals deserve special thanks:

- Phil Niekro, bullpen coordinator, Atlanta Braves
- Jim Small, Assistant Director of Public Relations, Major League Baseball
- Bill Guilfoile, Associate Director, Baseball Hall of Fame
- John Blake, Vice President, Public Relations, Texas Rangers
- Ned Colletti, Media Relations Director, Chicago Cubs
- Tim Mead, Director of Public Relations, California Angels
- Jim Schultz, Director of Public Relations, Atlanta Braves
- Larry Shenk, Vice President, Public Relations, Philadelphia Phillies
- Ed Lucas and Rich Marazzi, *Yankees Magazine*
- Kevin Barnes, freelance baseball writer and broadcaster, Atlanta, Ga.
- John Kuenster, editor, *Baseball Digest*
- Bruce Campbell and Bill Lawson, Insty-Prints, Clifton, N.J.

And finally, thanks to our player models: Michael Onyon, Erik Schirmer, Danielle Schleede, Katrina Wamsley, Stephen Whitaker, and Stephen Williams.

CONTENTS

CHAPTER 1

Finding the Road to Success

The desire to play baseball has been an American dream for more than a century. Nearly every young ballplayer dreams of becoming a major league star.

If you're like the vast majority of aspiring young players, you probably like to think of yourself as the center of attention—on the pitcher's mound. You get up there on that mound of dirt and suddenly everything seems to be revolving around you. You're the kingpin, the player everyone in the stands and on both teams is watching closely.

What makes pitching seem so attractive? There's a tension, an electricity that runs between the pitcher's mound and home plate. What's the pitcher going to throw? What's the hitter looking for? The catcher knows the particular strength and weakness of the batter as well as those of his pitcher; he is trying to work on the batter's weakness yet at the same time stay with the pitcher's strength, the pitch he throws best. The contest between pitcher and batter is like a game of chess, an intricate, complex game within the larger game of baseball. A batter is the focus of attention one time in nine of his team's plate appearances; the pitcher is always *there*, ball in hand. Standing on the mound in a big league stadium is the stuff of dreams.

Dreaming about becoming a major league pitcher is one thing. Actually doing it is something else. It's not something that just happens. It takes a lot of natural ability, a lot of dedication, enthusiasm, and hard work. It's not easy to determine early on if you've got the necessary talents. And as important as natural ability may be, it's nothing without dedication and, frankly, some measure of luck.

It helps to have support and encouragement from your parents, your coach, your friends. If they believe in you, if they want you to succeed and they let you know their feelings, it really helps. But in the end what matters is not whether you make it to "The Show," as the pros call the big leagues—very few young players do. The important thing is to become the best pitcher you can be, and not to give yourself the chance to say, years later, that you fell short because you didn't try hard enough.

In his formative years, every young pitcher must achieve the four C's of pitching: confidence, concentration, control, and consistency. Confidence is crucial, and must be attained first. An interested but patient parent can be a tremendous plus, but ultimately the pace and degree of your progress are up to you. The road to success is paved with good intentions and, even more important, good attention—to detail, to coaches, to the task at hand, and to your body.

What the coaches say

SPARKY ANDERSON Young kids should just play. Parents should let their children be kids. If they're good enough, they'll go on to professional ball. If they aren't, there's no way you're going to make them good enough.

I could teach a kid ten hours a day from the time he's 6 years old until he's 18, but he may not be able to play because God didn't gift him with that ability. Another kid might never talk to anybody about baseball but become a great player because of his natural ability.

Sparky Anderson advises parents just to let their children play ball without being pushed. Only their own talent and drive will make them stars.

BILLY GARDNER I don't think parents should push their kids. Kids have to find out for themselves if they want to play. If you push a boy, he'll resent you and the game.

What the pitchers say

STEVE CARLTON I developed my own style. Maybe young hitters can copy big league stars, but pitchers have to develop their own techniques.

I thought Sandy Koufax was the perfect pitcher from a mechanical standpoint. But there was no way I could throw the same way. You just can't copy another pitcher.

ROLLIE FINGERS Every kid I've ever known wanted to play Little League baseball. As a Little Leaguer, you just go out with the kids, play, and have a good time. The older you get, if you're good enough, you dedicate yourself to the game and go from there. But it takes a lot of dedication and a lot of time.

DWIGHT GOODEN My father helped me become a ballplayer. He taught me to take the good with the bad, learn from your mistakes, and come back the next day. My mom helped me a lot with my attitude problems and temper by talking to me about how people are watching you all the time and how stupid you make yourself look when you let your temper go.

I thought I was the best player on the [Hillsborough High School] team, and maybe I wouldn't have worked so hard if [coach Billy Reed] had let me coast. But he never let me rest on how good I thought I was. He never made me feel irreplaceable....He made me a better player without ever knocking down my confidence.

Dwight Gooden's father gave him some sound advice: learn from your mistakes.

PHIL NIEKRO There were a lot of better athletes in high school, and later in the minor leagues. I did not throw hard and I knew my fastball wasn't going to get me to the big leagues. I didn't have a good slider or good breaking ball either, but I knew my knuckleball was a little out of the ordinary and I could make it by perfecting the pitch and working on some other things.

I had to prepare myself physically and mentally. To me, the pitcher's mound became my house, my responsibility. When I released the ball to the catcher, I was no longer a pitcher—I was an infielder. When I got to the plate, I never felt I was a pitcher hitting—I felt I was a hitter batting in the ninth spot. I wanted to be the best bunter on the ballclub. When I got on base, I was a baserunner.

When a guy walked up to the plate, I had one job: to get the batter out. If he got to first base, I tried to keep him from scoring. I never looked at the second inning until I got by the first. The eighth or ninth inning was not important until I got there. If I was able to do what I had to do when I had to do it, I often found myself in the seventh, eighth, or ninth. But I never let my head get clouded by the future.

NOLAN RYAN My first organized sports experience was in Little League. The first field in Alvin [Texas] was cleared and built by my dad and the other fathers of the kids in the program. I played Little League from the time I was 9 until I was 13.

As a Little League parent, my dad was always there when I needed him, but he was not like some of the others you hear about—the kind who meddle in games and care more about their kids winning than how they play the game. My dad was just interested in my having a good organized sports experience.

Fireballing reliever Rob Dibble has fanned batters at a faster clip than anyone in baseball history—but fast though his pitches are, he depends more on movement than sheer velocity.

CHAPTER 2

A Scientific Approach to Pitching

If you want to learn how to pitch, you've got to start with the basics. If you understand the physics of baseball, especially the physics of pitching, you'll often be a step ahead of your rivals.

As a pitcher, you're an individual—you differ from every other pitcher in terms of your size, shape, ability, and many other factors. Each baseball is also one-of-a-kind. A ball is required to have a minimum circumference of 9 inches and a minimum weight of 5 ounces but upward variations of a quarter-inch and a quarter-ounce, respectively, are permitted. (A fastball pitcher is happy when he gets a smaller, heavier ball in his hand—it feels like a stone in a slingshot.) There are 108 stitches on a ball but neither machine nor human can sew them exactly the same way each time. Sometimes individual stitches or even entire seams are higher than others—a small difference but one that can be exploited by the clever pitcher, who will place maximum pressure on the raised portion of the seam to increase friction on the pitch, tightening its spin and thus increasing the sharpness of its movement.

Even though both the American and National leagues get their baseballs from the same source—and both require umpires to apply Lena Blackburne's Baseball Rubbing Mud before games to make them less slick—baseballs are as diverse as snowflakes. Even the same ball reacts differently each time it is thrown, because of such accidental alterations as grass stains or scuffs on the surface resulting from foul tips. The scuff, or stain, or dent—or, for that matter, the pressure applied by the fingers—increases the air resistance on that portion of the ball, thus altering the aerodynamic balance of the pitch. In other words, if the scuff or finger pressure is on the right side of the ball, the increased air resistance on that side makes the ball veer to the left, following the path of least resistance.

When you throw it, a baseball is subjected to friction caused by a meeting of its stitched surface and the air around it. Balls thrown hard meet more turbulence (that is, permit less action by the air around it) and begin to curve later than balls thrown at slower speeds: the flight path is determined by the spin. Though some scientists (if not many baseball people) dispute the assertion, a fastball can,

The last-minute rise on Nolan Ryan's fastball is really a gradual climb that can't be detected by the batter's eye.

if thrown with enough force and backspin, rise. The baseball overcomes the gravitational pull to earth just as an airplane takes the benefit of combined air resistance and pressure to generate lift. The rise seems sudden—the "hop" on a Nolan Ryan fastball, for instance—but in fact it is steady; the elevation just seems to be late, zooming above the batter's swing—because the eye cannot focus fast enough to follow a 90-m.p.h. "heater" from the pitcher's hand. In fact, even an ordinary fastball can present the illusion of rising simply because it defies gravity (falls, in plain English) more slowly than a breaking pitch or straight changeup.

The distance from the pitching rubber to home plate is set at 60'6", but allowing for a four-foot stride by a major league pitcher, the distance that the ball travels from the point of release is only about 56 feet. A fastball thrown 90 m.p.h. travels 132 feet per second and takes about 0.42 seconds to reach the center of home plate. A bat takes 0.20 seconds to get to the same place—creating a two-foot-wide "window" through which the ball passes in .015 of a second. As the pitcher, you can stand there on the mound, watching the catcher's signals, thinking about what you're going to do for ten or twenty seconds or so, but the batter has to react like lightning once you hurl your missile.

According to retired Stanford University physics professor Dr. Paul Kirkpatrick, there are twenty-six variables in space and time that dictate the success or failure rate of a batter. You don't need to know exactly what all those variables are for the purposes of this book, but they include adjustments to the speed, spin, movement, and location of the pitch, factors which you, the pitcher, have within your grasp. A batter is at a substantial disadvantage in the matchup against a pitcher: he must, with his round bat, make solid contact with a round ball—and even if he succeeds in this, he still must risk having a fielder record a hard-hit out.

After all, a first-rate hitter is defined as one who bats .300, which means that he fails in his mission seven times out of ten. (A pitcher who failed to record an out seven times in ten would not remain a pitcher for long!) You enjoy an enormous advantage over the batter. Remember that fact, and gain confidence from it. Don't pitch "too fine," and don't give in to the batter—the ball is in your hand, and he can't do a thing until you decide what you want to do with it.

A batter expecting a fastball can be badly fooled if you throw a slow curve instead. It's a matter of physics. Fastballs just don't behave the way curves do.

According to Robert K. Adair in *The Physics of Baseball*, a widebreaking curve thrown at 70 m.p.h. with a spin rate of 1,600 revolutions per minute and aimed at the inside corner of the plate must break 14.4 inches to pass over the outside corner. Yet the largest deviation of the pitch from a straight line, beginning to end, is in truth only 3.4 inches. What this means is that, as may happen with the fastball, we have another illusion—to the batter, the ball seems to curve a lot more than it really does. And of course, how the batter sees the ball and how he reacts to a pitch are dependent, in part, on what he is expecting to see. And besides, 3.4 inches can mean the difference between a solid hit and a clear miss. There is a science to pitching, clearly, but you don't have to be a great scientist to be a great pitcher: there is art, too, and more than a little bit of magic, or sleight of hand.

That is why "scientific" attempts to measure pitcher skill, such as scouts using radar guns to time pitching prospects, are surely overemphasized. Though some scouts live by the gun, other baseball insiders don't like it. Knowledgeable evaluators of pitching talent know that a 92-m.p.h. heater that is as straight as a string is far easier to hit than an 85-m.p.h. fastball that moves. Velocity is a great asset—

it's a gift, and it can't be taught—but it is not as important as movement or location. As an aspiring major leaguer, you can only hope that those who are evaluating your performance using a radar gun will realize both its value and its limitations.

At all levels of baseball, from Little League to the big leagues, pitching speeds vary widely. The hard thrower may command the headlines, but the pitcher with guile and command—and an arsenal of tricks—can be just as successful. Whichever kind of pitcher you may become, you'll need to have confidence that your fastball can get batters out, whatever its speed. And by understanding the basic principles of physics that we've just discussed, you can gain that confidence, readying yourself for your development from a thrower to a pitcher.

What the coaches say

BOB FELLER All the radar gun gives you is velocity. It doesn't tell you the movement of the ball. Most people who've got two good eyes can sit there and see if a guy can throw hard and what the ball is doing.

WHITEY HERZOG Radar guns are good when they tell you the guy starts the game throwing 90 m.p.h. and slows down to 86 by the sixth inning. But scouts should never rely on them as their sole source of evaluating a young pitcher. Guns don't tell you anything about motion or delivery—and they don't tell you whether a pitcher is going to get better as he matures. If scouts had used a radar gun before they signed Catfish Hunter, he never would have gone pro.

Whitey Herzog, former manager of the St. Louis Cardinals, believes that the exclusive use of radar guns by scouts in judging prospects could prevent deserving players from reaching the professional ranks.

Roger Clemens of the Boston Red Sox—a beautiful blending of power and finesse.

CHAPTER 3

Proper Mechanics

It's important for you to understand the physics of baseball, but there is other basic ground to be covered as well. Without the proper mechanics, you'll never become a winner. By "mechanics" we mean the basic kinds of skills you've got to master before and during the act of firing that ball toward the plate.

First you need to become familiar with your workplace: the mound and the pitching rubber.

The Workplace

The mound is an elevated dirt area no more than 10 inches high at its peak. The pitcher's area wasn't always an elevated mound. When major league baseball officially began with the launch of the National League in 1876, pitchers delivered the ball underhanded from a flat surface within a box, the front of which was only 45 feet from home plate. This is why pitchers are sometimes "knocked out of the box.") The idea of a raised area was introduced sometime in the mid-1880s, once overhand pitching was legalized, to give the pitcher more power over batters. The slab was added in 1893, at which time the pitching distance was set at the present 60'6". The exact height of the mound, originally set at 15 inches but largely unmonitored, was reduced to its present level after pitchers had come to dominate the game in the major leagues in 1968.

From the Little League to the majors, no pitcher can be successful unless he's comfortable on the mound. And that may require a certain amount of housekeeping or excavation—not only before every game but before every inning. Your pitching opponent may be a bit taller or shorter than you, may have a longer or shorter stride, and may plant his front foot in a position that is comfortable for him but represents a potential hazard for you. You've got to be very meticulous.

Pebbles that could cause bad hops must be removed, holes dug by the opposing pitcher must be repaired, and potentially dangerous areas of mud must be obliterated by careful landscaping. If you stride into the mud while making a delivery, you not only could look foolish but you could also be seriously hurt.

The pitching rubber, a slab secured at the peak of the mound, is 24 inches long and 6 inches wide. You've got to begin your pitch with your back foot in contact with the rubber: that's the rule, and thus a part of basic pitching mechanics. You can take a position anywhere along the length of the rubber, and it's a good idea for a beginning pitcher not to move along the rubber from batter to batter. You should find the spot on the rubber where you're most comfortable and stay with that one spot. Top major league pitchers, almost all of whom throw with a full overhand or three-quarters delivery, usually pitch from the middle of the rubber. If you stand directly on top of the rubber, however, you're not going to have a good base for pushing off. If you stand too much to the side, you could be hurting your game by dropping your arm below your elbow—in effect throwing only with your forearm.

As you advance in confidence and skill, you may one day choose to vary your position for lefthanded and righthanded batters. For example, a righthanded pitcher throwing with a sidearm delivery to a righthanded batter can achieve a nasty crossfire effect—appearing to be throwing almost from third base—by positioning his back foot at the extreme right of the rubber. A righthander might also consider moving to the left side of the rubber against a lineup loaded with lefthanded batters; such a move gives the lefthanded batter a less clear look at the ball as it leaves the pitcher's hand, making it tougher for him to identify what kind of pitch it is from its rotation.

In the housekeeping line, pay special attention to the rubber. Be sure it is anchored securely into the

Find a spot on the mound where you feel comfortable. Most major leaguers start from the center of the rubber.

In certain situations, you can move to one side of the rubber or the other to be a more effective pitcher.

ground and that the dirt around it has not eroded, leaving a hole that might snare your spikes. The rubber shouldn't move when you shove off; an unstable rubber can lead to a wrenched arm or leg.

The Pitching Position

When you're comfortable on the mound, you're ready to pitch. There are two basic pitching positions: the windup position and the set position (which, when combined with an upward movement of the arms, is called the stretch position). You can use either of them at any time—though the set or stretch position makes sense when runners are on base.

Pitching from the windup position takes more time because the whole body is involved to a greater extent than with the set position. The windup gives you more momentum and velocity, but sometimes less control, because there are more things that can go wrong with a complex delivery than with a simple one. Because the windup is slow to unfold, and difficult to break off in mid-motion for a legal pickoff attempt, the windup also would allow baserunners to get a better jump toward the next base; this is why the set position is preferred when men are on base.

Pitching from the windup position, your first responsibility is to keep the ball hidden from the batter and the baseline coaches. While leaning in to take the sign from the catcher, a righthanded pitcher should place his pitching hand in the glove, his right (pivot) foot on the rubber, and his left foot four to six inches behind it. Another option, open to southpaws as well as righties, is placing both feet on the rubber if this seems a more comfortable starting point.

Although we will analyze the distinct components of the full motion in detail later in the chapter, the windup delivery proceeds like this: With both arms dangling in front of the body, the pitcher holds the ball firmly in the mitt with his right hand. He should be gripping the ball not too tightly, not too loosely. Don't place the ball far back in the hand, unless you're throwing a changeup. The righthanded pitcher begins his motion: moving his weight back on his left foot, bringing his hands above his head, and pausing for at least one full second before bringing the right arm behind the back as he strides toward the batter with his left foot. He pivots as he steps forward, with his left shoulder and left side facing the batter, then finishes the throw by turning his chest and body toward the hitter—placing himself in good fielding position.

Because of the sight of swirling arms and legs, pitching from the windup position may disrupt the batter's concentration—which from your point of view is certainly a good thing. But an improper or overly elaborate windup may also hurt the pitcher, causing problems with balance and coordination that may not only impair control but may also lead to long-term arm trouble.

For that reason, some pitchers prefer a no-windup delivery—eliminating the step back, the pump, and the overhead arm motion. You may experiment with

When leaning in to get a sign from your catcher, remember to keep the ball hidden in your glove.

The pitching motion begins by moving your weight onto your left leg, if you are a righty.

As the motion continues, bring your hands above your head, where you pause for one second before your right arm goes behind your back.

For the righthander, the set position begins with the right foot along the edge of the rubber.

In the set position, a righthander's body faces third base, with his left side facing the batter.

both approaches and decide what is best for you, but pitching from a full windup does build rhythm, getting your legs and back into the pitch and so adding several miles per hour to its speed. Don't be hasty to decide that a windup is not for you, even if you find control much easier to master from a set position.

The set position produces a more compact delivery, taking less time and offering greater control. It requires more of a push-off but less of a kick and pivot than the windup position.

For a righthander, the set position begins with the right hand at his side and the sole of the right foot along the front edge of the rubber (the foot can be in front of the rubber as long as the little-toe side of the shoe is touching it). The left foot is parallel to the right foot and less than six inches in front of it.

Instead of facing the batter directly, as in the windup position, the righthanded pitcher working from the set position faces third base, with his left side facing the batter. If he decides to come home, he takes a short stride, pivots on his right foot, and turns his chest toward the hitter as he releases the ball.

You can combine the set position with the stretch position, which allows you to stretch your arms slowly above your head, bring them down to chest level, and pause to check the leads of the baserunners (this pause is known as "coming set"). But you've got to be careful when doing this. It'll be a balk if you don't come to a complete stop. (Because of the required return to the set position, the stretch position differs from the continuous motion of the windup position.)

The Pitching Motion

Proper pitching motion permits the pitcher to get maximum movement, velocity, and location out of each pitch. From the windup position, there are five components to the motion: stance, step back (pump), pivot, stride, and follow-through. The release of the pitch comes after the stride and before the follow-through.

Some pitching motions are very distinctive. Hall of Famers Warren Spahn and Juan Marichal, for example, intimidated batters with abnormally high leg kicks when working with the bases empty. Fernando Valenzuela breaks eye contact with the catcher at the apex of his motion. Copying such exaggerated styles is not recommended, especially for beginners, but mastering the fundamentals of mechanics is.

The mechanics of motion begin with a good stance, which gives you the balance you need for a smooth delivery. A righthander should keep his weight forward on his right leg, while keeping the trailing (left) leg flexible. The ball should be held behind the back or in the glove (with the ball and glove hand joined) so that the batter won't know what's coming. Stare in at the catcher to pick up the sign, and maintain eye contact with your target (the catcher's glove); you're not Fernando.

Lefthander Fernando Valenzuela of the Los Angeles Dodgers often fails to keep his eye on the catcher's glove.

The step back or pump is part of the rocking motion that begins the windup. While keeping the right foot on the rubber, the righthander steps straight back—not sideways!—with his left foot and places his weight on that foot. The hands come forward, brushing past the hips, until the ball and glove meet over the pitcher's head. The step and arm motion finish simultaneously.

On the pivot , the pitcher turns his trailing foot (the right foot for a righthander) clockwise so that it is parallel to the rubber—without lifting it off the rubber—and transfers his full weight to that foot. If the pivot is done correctly, the hitter will see the pitcher's back pocket. At the end of the pivot, a righthander's right foot points toward third base—perpendicular to its original position.

The nonpitching hip and shoulder now face home plate. The pitcher brings his lead leg up (the left side for a righthanded pitcher), bends his trailing (right) knee a little, and brings his hands down to knee level. When they meet, the pitcher pulls them apart (breaks the hands) and moves the pitching hand behind the hip. The shoulders remain parallel to the ground at all times.

The righthanded pitcher takes his stride (an average of about four to four-and-a-half feet) by aiming his airborne left foot toward home plate. He brings the front shoulder forward, swings the pitching arm back, and lifts the pitching elbow slightly above the shoulder. He should be especially careful not to hook his arm before releasing the pitch. After pushing off the rubber with the right leg (bent at the knee), he lands firmly on the full left foot (not the heel), with the toes pointed toward the plate.

To release, or deliver, the ball, the pitcher moves his arm in a complete circle, keeping the elbow above the shoulder. (This is the rule for an overhand or three-quarters delivery, but not for sidearm.) Don't drop that elbow, and don't let the elbow get ahead of your wrist—that will result in your pushing, or short-arming, a soft pitch up to the plate that will be clobbered.

The ball is released with a snap of the wrist—keep it loose!—from a point about a foot over the pitcher's head and a foot past his ear (in a three-quarters delivery). Every pitch should be released from the same point. Varying your release points will harm your control and may serve to tip batters off to your pitches.

As he releases the ball, the pitcher now concerns himself with the follow-through. He brings his right foot around and plants it slightly forward of his left foot, perhaps twenty-four inches apart from it but almost in parallel. Your left foot should land twelve inches to the left of its starting point. If it lands even with or to the right of that point, your arm and body movements are unsynchronized and your weight is not properly distributed. As a result, your pitches will lack both velocity and control.

The follow-through is complete when the pitcher brings his pitching hand across the midline of his body toward his glove-side ankle (the left ankle for a righthander). He must permit the force of his arm motion to pull him around; a sudden stop after the release of the pitch could hurt his arm.

Bend your back as you release the pitch; staying straight up deprives you of power. And keep your front leg flexible as you deliver to the plate. Not doing that invites arm and shoulder injuries and is one of the fundamental mechanical mistakes pitchers make (a righthanded pitcher gets his power from his right, or rear, leg but puts the full pressure of each pitch on the left, or front, leg).

Follow-through is important because a pitcher must be in the proper position to make fielding plays—or at least to protect himself from a hard line drive hit directly at him. Many pitchers, however, find that following through is difficult for them.

In fact, not all pitchers take an orthodox approach to follow-through. One of the game's greatest pitchers, Bob Gibson of the St. Louis Cardinals, was so off-balance in his follow-through that he often fell off the mound after delivering a pitch. But he refused to risk losing any of the power in his explosive delivery. If you throw hard, you should not be concerned about losing velocity in order to field your position. Even though it seems that there are as many individualized pitching motions in the major leagues as there are pitchers, many fine pitchers use traditional techniques of motion and follow-through.

The Delivery

The actual act of throwing the ball is a directional skill first. After your trailing leg swings forward, however, it's a rotational skill. Your body positions the arm and then your arm positions the ball. At least, that's the idea behind sound mechanics. Once you get the hang of it, it comes naturally—but you've got to really work at it to get your throwing arm and body to function together. For example, by turning his left shoulder and left leg in the direction of his throw, a righthanded pitcher generates considerable power from his back and shoulder muscles; if he fails to pivot fully, he loses velocity. The same is true if he "opens up" too soon (his left shoulder flying out toward first base while his arm is trailing) or not enough, so that he is throwing across his body. In either case, his pitch is thrown "with his arm," rather than with his entire body.

There are many ways to throw a baseball, but only three basic deliveries: overhand, three-quarters, and sidearm. A handful of established pitchers also use a submarine, or underhand, delivery. All these deliveries can be employed from either a windup or a set position.

Many coaches insist that the overhand delivery is best because it allows the pitcher to use the full power of his shoulders. For beginning pitchers— or, indeed, any beginning player who wants to develop his arm strength to the maximum—many instructors insist upon an overhand motion. Throwing three-quarters or sidearm at an early age, they say, leads to shortened muscle structures and bad habits.

Even for the older pitcher-in-training, it would be wise to remember that batters find it more difficult to gauge the vertical motion of a pitch than its lateral, or side-to-side, movement. Only a full overhand delivery can produce a curveball with an awesome drop like that of Baltimore's Gregg Olson. Moreover, a pitcher who delivers "straight over the top" offers no advantage to opposite-side hitters (lefthanded hitters against righthanded pitchers, righthanded hitters against lefthanded pitchers); as mentioned earlier, a righthanded sidearmer gives a lefthanded batter a clear look at the ball, all the way from his hand to the plate.

Throwing overhand gives maximum arm extension and drop, so the temptation is to raise the arm as high as possible. However, your elbow must be bent slightly, if not as much as in a three-quarters delivery. Flipping a pitch straight-armed toward the batter will deprive you of the force of your legs and back muscles, producing a lifeless fastball. As you open up (presuming a righthanded pitcher), there should be a pronounced tilt of your left shoulder down to first base—about 45 degrees off the horizontal plane. Your right shoulder, in line with third base, will be tilted up about 45 degrees.

Questions of spin aside, the ball does sail in straight from an overhand delivery, while it comes in at an angle from the three-quarters style, adding one more element of deception for the batter to contend with. The pitch delivered three-quarters

The overhand delivery is preferred by many coaches because it allows a pitcher to use the full power of his shoulder.

also sinks, sails, or tails more easily, even though its side-to-side movement exceeds its drop. Generally speaking, however, balls that move laterally as well as vertically are harder to hit. For these reasons, the three-quarters delivery is used most often by big leaguers.

In a three-quarters delivery the elbow is bent more than in the overhand delivery, so that the forearm and upper arm almost form an L shape. The shoulders are not quite parallel, but the tilt toward first base is nowhere near as pronounced as in the overhand delivery.

Sidearm pitchers are particularly tough on same-side hitters. What the sidearm pitcher may lose in velocity or in the drop on his curveball, he gains in intimidation. And there are few pitches more intimidating than a rapidly sinking sidearm fastball. It takes plenty of nerve for a batter to hold his

ground in the batter's box against a sidearm pitch that seems aimed directly at him, not the plate.

The sidearm delivery requires shoulders that are parallel to the ground and an elbow that is only slightly bent. The body does not drive toward the plate the way it does with an overhand or three-quarters delivery, and thus the speed and movement of the ball are imparted almost entirely by the whip of the arm. For this reason, a sidearm delivery is not recommended to young pitchers as their dominant delivery, even though it produces little strain on the arm.

Like the sidearm pitch, the submarine delivery causes a drop in pitching velocity. But the delivery baffles batters who are not used to seeing it. It's not that sidearmers are so difficult for catchers to handle, but coaches don't like to see young pitchers throw submarine-style because it is does so little

The three-quarter delivery is used most often by major league pitchers because pitches come in at an angle.

Throwing sidearm may result in a loss of velocity and downward movement, but it also increases intimidation.

to tax young muscles that are in need of development.

Sidearm and submarine pitches are hard to control, especially if you're not used to pitching them. You should not experiment with them in a tight situation with men on base, when control is crucial.

Common Problems

Even the greatest major league pitchers have bad outings and periodic problems with their pitching mechanics. These problems may be mental or physical, or a combination of the two. They include:

- rushing
- overstriding
- overthrowing
- short-arming
- failing to look at the target
- improper follow-through
- throwing across the body
- placing an improper grip on the ball
- tipping off pitches

Rushing caused Hall of Famer Lefty Grove to lose control of his fastball on occasion. In an effort to overcome this, Connie Mack, his manager on the Philadelphia Athletics, made Grove count to ten before he pitched. Rivals and fans who heard about this tried to upset the great lefthander by counting out loud when he was on the mound. But the tactic failed. Grove was too wise in the ways of the game to fall for it.

A pitcher who rushes his motion loses control and risks injury. If he rushes only in certain situations—such as when men are on base, or the score is tight and the inning late—then he might conclude that nerves and trying too hard are the causes. If he rushes only in the late innings when fatigue sets in, he will need to maintain his concentration and monitor his mechanics more closely. Learning his tendencies is the first step, and for this an observant coach is indispensable.

Most often, rushing is not a product of anxiety but simply the display of one or more bad habits that a pitcher slips into unknowingly, like keeping the weight on his left foot too long during the windup.

Relief ace Jeff Reardon ocassionally overthrows the ball, which results in many of his pitches coming in high.

Young pitchers are especially susceptible to lapses in their mechanics for the simple reason that they have had fewer years in which to master them, to make them a constant whenever they pitch.

Whatever part of your motion is most recently learned or most flawed is the one that will slide first—and because a sound pitching motion consists of many integrated actions, one flaw will inevitably lead to another. If your glove-side leg kicks too far back at the height of your windup, your pitching arm will trail your body and legs and your rhythm will be shot. Velocity will drop as your delivery becomes "all arm." Rushing is the pitcher's natural attempt to have some parts of his motion catch up with those that have jumped out too soon.

Rushing, after all, is only the visible symptom of one or more smaller problems; it is not something you can remedy directly. It's as if someone said "your problem is that you are nervous." True

Putting it all together—lefthanded

The motion begins with the weight on your left leg as you look in for your sign.

Your weight is then transferred to your right leg as both hands come above your head, where they pause for a moment.

During the pivot all weight is placed on the left foot, which is parallel to the rubber. The right leg kicks about waist high.

Pushing off his left foot, the pitcher then strides; his left arm is directly behind him, ready to throw the ball.

After landing on his right foot, the pitcher releases the ball when it is about a foot above his head and a foot past his left ear.

In the follow-through, the left arm continues forward and finishes with the elbow nearly touching the right knee.

Putting it all together—righthanded

The motion begins with the weight on your right leg as you look in for your sign.

Your weight is then transferred to your left leg as both hands come above your head, where they pause for a moment.

During the pivot all weight is placed on the right foot, which is parallel to the rubber. The left leg kicks about waist high.

Pushing off his right foot, the pitcher then strides; his right arm is directly behind him, ready to throw the ball.

After landing on his left foot, the pitcher releases the ball when it is about a foot above his head and a foot past his right ear.

In the follow-through, the right arm continues forward and finishes with the elbow nearly touching the left knee.

enough, perhaps, but to correct your nervousness we would have to determine what it was that made you nervous, and try to remedy that. There is no set drill that will correct rushing: it is the product of a loss of concentration, and the antidote for that is to loosen up and relax on the mound. Slow down your delivery. Baseball games have innings, not time periods. There's no clock ticking away, no buzzer getting ready to blare.

If your windup is too fast or too slow, your pitches will be too high or too low or too wide or too slow. A windup that is out of synch may also cause you to overstride or understride .

Overstriding can also result from a poorly maintained mound. If there's a hole in the dirt and you step into it while winding up, it may alter your usual motion. Most often, though, stride problems are the result of pitching motions that are newly learned or have had new elements added to them. You may not yet have determined the length of stride that is comfortable for you and produces good results. If your pitchers are consistently coming in high, you might try lengthening your stride; if they are consistently low, you are probably overstriding and need to shorten up.

Overthrowing produces the high pitches that most batters like. If you overthrow, the probable cause is simple: you're just trying too hard. Again, the best advice is: relax. Stay within yourself. An increase in effort does not necessarily lead to a gain in speed, and it may very well reduce the movement of your pitches. And remember: Even if *you* don't have confidence in your stuff, *the batters* are going to fail seven times out of ten.

Short-arming occurs if you don't fully extend your throwing arm, causing you to lose the power normally provided by the long natural arc of a throw. It can be the result of falling behind in the count and aiming the ball in hopes of a strike, or after a couple of walks have eroded a pitcher's confidence.

Correcting mechanical flaws is best done by pitching, pitching, and more pitching, on the sidelines under the watchful eye of a coach. But mistakes can often be corrected during a game. It's all too easy to start doing something wrong without being aware of it. If you don't correct your mistakes

as you go along, your catcher or pitching coach can sometimes be quick to spot a flaw and let you know about it. Listen to them.

Looking at the target—the catcher's glove—is usually easy. If you start forgetting to do this, you'll definitely begin to have control problems. Have you begun to kick your raised front leg so far back toward the infield that your head turns away from the plate? Have you developed the habit of pitching to the batter instead of to your catcher? Concentrate.

An improper follow-through can damage your throwing arm, rob your pitch of steam and stuff, and leave you in a poor fielding position afterwards. If you fail to bend your back properly, or don't bring your arm down and across the midline of your body after the ball is released, you'll often foul up your follow-through, your pitch, and your arm.

At the end of the follow-through, your front foot should be pointed toward home plate. If it isn't, you'll find yourself dropping your arm and throwing across your body. A good way for you to avoid this problem is to imagine a seven-foot line on the ground from your pivot foot to home plate. If you're a righthander, at the end of your stride, your left foot should always be on the left side of the line.

Proper grip is also essential. It is important for you to grip the ball both correctly and comfortably. A grip that is too loose or too tight will cause control trouble, with a loose grip generally producing high pitches and a tight grip driving the pitches into the dirt. Correct this as you would with a problem in striding, by trial and error.

Another problem you may encounter is "telegraphing" or tipping off your pitches. This allows the hitter an edge and you lose the key advantage of mystery. If you continually make a distinctive movement that reveals what you're about to throw, you're giving the batter an extra advantage.

If you always raise your arms higher for a fastball than for a curve, you're sending batters a message. The same is true if you change your deliveries as you change pitches (sidearm for a curve, overhand for a fastball, etc.). Batters who know what's coming are much more likely to succeed.

When a pitcher's mechanics are working, he can pinpoint his pitches so well that the catcher hardly has to move his mitt. Nothing pleases a coach more, and nothing—neither speed nor stuff—goes so far toward success as control. It's a lot to master—the workplace, the pitching positions, the motions, the delivery, and above all the ability to concentrate.

Even pitchers at the top of their profession often have to get back to these basics when things go wrong. There's a lot more to learn about pitching, too, but you can't work on the top floors of the building until you've put in the foundation.

What the coaches say

MEL STOTTLEMYRE When a pitcher gets into the heat of a battle, with two or three men on, he may stiffen his wrist and throw the ball a little harder. He'll drop his elbow and push the baseball or drag his arm and sling the ball.

Maintaining a nice, loose wrist allows good ball movement and gets that little extra on the fastball without having to overthrow. A pitcher should not let himself tense, tighten up, and squeeze the baseball. That kills all flexibility in the wrist, which is one of the most important levers we have in proper throwing.

Doug Drabek of the Pittsburgh Pirates maintains his control by continuously concentrating on the catcher's mitt.

JEFF TORBORG Nolan Ryan has the perfect combination of factors needed to throw a baseball at a very high velocity. He has the proper release point, a balanced follow-through, and the retention of weight on the rubber. And he does it without having anything extraordinary, like Sandy Koufax's large hands that made his curveball drop a mile.

What the pitchers say

DOUG DRABEK Control is good concentration on the mitt. You've seen major league pitchers who turn their heads away before throwing, but they're older guys who've had a long time to learn how to pitch. At your level, keep your eye on that catcher's mitt.

TOM SEAVER I learned from hard experience that the higher you go on the baseball ladder, the more batters will take advantage of your mistakes. Nobody is perfect and we all make mistakes. But our goal must be not to repeat them.

You can't concentrate on mechanics while you're pitching—you should be doing things automatically. I never visualized myself in the act of pitching. I only visualized the spot where I wanted the ball to end up.

DAVE STIEB [After elbow problems forced me to replace the slider with a curve in 1986,] my stride had gotten away from what it used to be. I was striding too much toward third base and throwing a bit across my body. I tried to stride straight toward the plate, even a little bit toward first. I also had to adjust the angle of my arm. I looked at films from 1985, when I pitched well, and discovered my arm had dropped down.

Maybe it was the result of my elbow problem.

I changed the way I stepped with my left foot. I used to land with a stiff leg and there was a certain amount of recoil. I concentrated on bending the leg, to land more softly. I also had to find a more consistent release point and change my follow-through.

I had to incorporate all these things every time I threw a pitch and also worry about location. It took a lot of hard work over a period of time. [After he made the changes, Stieb was suddenly an All-Star again. Opposing batters, baffled by his hard curve, believed that he had resurrected his slider, but he had simply overhauled his mechanics.]

Striding too much toward third base caused Dave Stieb to throw across his body. By correcting this and some other mechanical problems, he soon returned to All Star status.

CHAPTER 4

Pitches You Can Throw Now

To win as a pitcher, you need to be in command of several different pitches. The choices vary widely, but coaches and trainers insist that young pitchers throw only fastballs and changeups until their growing arms have matured. We know that you'll fool around in the backyard with a curveball or knuckler at an early age, and we will satisfy your curiosity about how such pitches are thrown and what makes them behave in the ways they do—but *don't* work on breaking pitches extensively, or use them in game situations, without the approval of your coach and/or doctor. *We cannot emphasize this strongly enough.*

Throwing curves, screwballs, and sliders at this point in your life poses a very real threat of injury to your arm, and besides, it keeps you from mastering the fastballs and changeups you need to succeed in various organized youth leagues. Premature reliance upon breaking pitches can also stunt the development of your arm strength, depriving you—perhaps forever—of the velocity you can achieve only by throwing fastballs, fastballs, and more fastballs.

Nonetheless, we will cover the full arsenal available to college-age players and the pros so you will know about these pitches when your physique and your foundation in the basics permit an advance to the breaking pitches. These pitches are more physically demanding and fraught with peril because they place unusual strains on the elbow, wrist, and shoulder—or, in the case of the forkball, the tendons in the fingers.

How old should you be before working seriously on a curve or other breaking pitch? Most trainers and big-league pitchers say 14, but others advise waiting until 16. And some major league organizations have adopted the position that especially demanding pitches like the slider be prohibited even for their minor-league pitchers; in their view, mastery of a fastball, change, and curve are enough to get you to "The Show."

On the college and professional levels, a starter needs to master at least three pitches because he faces each opposing hitter at least three times in a game. A long reliever, who may face each opposing hitter twice, may be able to get by with two pitches, but inside every long reliever is a starter just hoping to break into the rotation; he had better have three pitches, too. A short reliever, likely to see each enemy hitter once in a one- or two-inning stint, can be comfortable with mastery of a single pitch. Another consideration for a short reliever is that he often comes in with men on base or when allowing a run will lose the ballgame. For him, keeping men off the bases is imperative, and it is harder to establish equal measures of control for three pitches while warming up in the bullpen than it is for only one.

The three basic pitches are the fastball, the breaking ball (curveball or slider), and the changeup. They are the pitches used to judge pitching hopefuls at big college baseball programs like the one at the University of Arizona; coaches there consider it a bonus if anyone is able to throw more difficult pitches. On the other hand, major league scouts checking out prospects of the same age (18 or so) place much more emphasis on the fastball and good mechanics.

Setting up the hitter is not only the major league baseball way to pitch, but a strategy that begins in Little League. Before a pitcher can select his arsenal, he needs to consider all possible options, although no pitcher should consider ditching his fastball; it will always be the best pitch in baseball, and the basis for all the deceptive variations a pitcher may add as he matures. Even a pitcher like Bob Ojeda—who is not blessed with a 90-m.p.h. blazer and relies upon a great variety of changes of speed to keep batters off balance—records most of his outs with his fastball.

Building your arsenal means conducting a careful study of each pitch, what it can do, and how it can be thrown effectively. Throwing an array of different pitches at different speeds to different locations, while having a sequence or progression in mind before you throw the first ball to a particular batter—this is the art of pitching.

We'll take a look at all the pitches the big leaguers employ, covering first the pitches you can throw now: the fastball and changeup. In the next chapter we will review the various breaking pitches, starting with the curveball, that your age, physique, and experience may permit you to attempt later on.

Bobby Ojeda changes speeds on his pitches often to keep batters off balance.

Fastball

The fastball is the best pitch in baseball. Thrown properly, it is the easiest to control, most difficult for the batter to time, and the necessary complement to any or all of the breaking pitches. A good hitter may be described as being a "fastball hitter," but all that means is that he can get the bat around on a speedy mistake, one thrown to the wrong spot. *No one*—not Babe Ruth, not Ted Williams, not Jose Canseco—consistently hits a great fastball thrown up-and-in or low-and-away. And the fastball is the most forgiving of pitches: make a mistake and hang a curveball or slider and it'll be walloped, but if a fastball is sent in across the letters, the batter will more often than not simply pop it up.

Your fastball doesn't have to be as good as Dwight Gooden's or Nolan Ryan's for you to make it your bread-and-butter pitch. A fastball pitcher with good control will be extremely effective if he has at least one other pitch to keep the batters "honest" and throw off their timing.

And while in broad terms it is true that breaking pitches are learned and speed is a gift, you cannot afford to neglect your development of the fastball. Practice and study can pay off in added miles per hour and dramatically increased movement.

Don't think, by the way, that you have to be an imposing physical specimen to throw a good fastball! Slightly built major leaguers like Ramon Martinez or Tom Gordon notch plenty of K's because they have "live" arms, great wrist action, and good arm-body rhythm.

There are two types of fastball: the one that rises, or at least appears to rise because it loses altitude less quickly than pitches thrown more slowly; and the one that sinks or darts because it meets more air resistance. Both of these types of fastball may also be "cut"—not physically nicked or scuffed, but held with an off-center grip that exposes more of the laces on one side than the other. Indeed, the cut fastball behaves more like a slider, in that its "late-breaking" lateral movement is more important than its speed. An argument made on behalf of the cut fastball is that it gives a pitcher a slider while permitting him to throw without placing strain on his elbow, which a slider inevitably does. So although you may not yet be ready to throw a breaking pitch, you'll be amazed at how much movement you can obtain with your fastball simply by altering the position of the ball in your hand, or by rolling your fingers to the left (for a righthander, that is) at the point of release. This second type of fastball—the sinking, darting kind—cannot attain the velocity of the pure riser.

It is the rising fastball that you should attempt to develop as fully as you can, mixing in the sinking fastball or cut fastball to keep the hitter off balance. If you don't throw thousands and thousands of four-seamers in your formative years, you may never know how fast you could really throw. Some analysts of baseball in the last decade or so have remarked how there used to be more good fastball pitchers among the annual crop of prospects, and

in the major leagues themselves. They chalk this up to a variety of reasons, but a primary cause surely is that pitchers fall in love with sinkers and breaking pitches too early. The split-finger fastball may have been "the pitch of the '80s" at the major league level, but once the novelty began to wear off and the sore arms kicked in, managers and executives voiced the hope that the fastball would regain its preeminence in the 1990s.

No matter whether you throw the rising fastball (also known as a four-seam fastball) over the top, three-quarters, or sidearm, the grip is always the same. The ball is gripped across the long seams with the index and middle fingers spread three-quarters of an inch apart. The thumb supports the ball on one side and the ring finger on the other: the thumb puts pressure on the bottom seam, just as the index and middle fingers place pressure on the top seam; the ring finger simply provides a "ledge" or resting place for the ball, and does not come in contact with the seam.

Do not grip the ball too tightly, or too far back in the hand. You should see some space between the

The grip for the four-seam fastball.

The fastball should not be held too far back in your hand. There should be a small space between the ball and your palm as you hold it.

A sinking fastball is achieved by gripping the ball along the seams rather than across them.

ball and the "C" formed by the curve of your index finger and thumb. Make sure that while the fleshy tips of your index and middle fingers are pressed against the seam—*not* the extreme ends of the fingers—no pressure is exerted by the remaining length of those fingers; pressure of that kind will disperse or lessen the pressure on the seam and rob the fastball of rotation and lift.

When the four-seam fastball is released with an overhand delivery, all four seams spin backward toward the pitcher as he releases the ball by pulling down and across the top seam; the thumb provides a further push in the same manner. The effect is to make the ball spin upward. The individual pitcher's unique combination of arm action, fingertip pressure, and wrist snap determine the tightness of the rotation and thus the amount of "rise" in each pitch. When delivered three-quarters, the ball spins upward and tails (a fastball thrown by a righthander veers left). The more revolutions per minute ("r.p.m."), the more movement on the fastball—the

principle is the same for the curve or slider, by the way—and the more difficult it is for the batter to pick up the flight of the ball.

A four-seam fastball delivered overhand can be breathtaking if it is exceptionally fast because of the *swoosh* of its rise, like a jetliner taking off. But most fastball pitchers prefer the three-quarters delivery because it imparts additional lateral movement, giving the batter something else to which he must adjust.

The sinking fastball, or two-seam fastball, sinks because the ball meets more air resistance as the seams rotate less rapidly. The sinking fastball is released in the same manner as the rising fastball, with the index and middle fingers placing pressure on the top and the thumb on the underside. Unlike the riser, however, the sinker is gripped *along* the seams rather than across them; the seams are lined up vertically rather than horizontally.

In the cross-seam grip (the rising fastball), the rapid rotation of the seams lifts the ball. Pitches held across the seams always gain both rotation and speed.

But when the ball is gripped along the short, rounded seams (the sinking fastball), the slower rotation as the ball's unstitched surfaces spin plateward pulls the ball down. The fewer stitches presented to the air space between the pitcher and batter, the more that gravity and air pressure act on the ball.

Because of its tight rotation, the four-seam fastball looks "smaller" to the batter than a normal baseball. The seams spin so fast that they are hardly visible, making the ball appear to be a blur of white. At advanced levels of baseball, when batters must identify and react to pitches with lightning speed, they rely upon "reading" the rotation of the ball to determine what kind of pitch it is and where it will cross the plate. (Case in point: The slider is so tough to hit because its tight rotation makes it look, for nearly half the distance between mound and plate, just like a fastball—only then it makes a sudden, if small, break.) The two-seam fastball, which doesn't rotate as fast, permits the batter to pick up the red seams fairly easily; it must have good sinking action to avoid looking like a fat batting-practice pitch. Thrown well, the two-seamer usually induces the batter to hit the ball on the ground.

When a pitcher gets into trouble with his fastball it is not because it has become less fast, but because it has lost its accustomed movement. Seldom is the answer a flaw in the grip or anything else specific to the fastball. Almost always the problem goes back to basic mechanics: such things as understriding, overthrowing, or dropping the arm and leading with the elbow. The previous chapter offered the basics for success with any pitch. When things go wrong for you with a particular pitch like the fastball or changeup, get back to those basics and your "stuff" will magically return.

Because a good fastball has movement of one kind or another, it is, in effect, a "breaking" pitch. A pitcher with a moving fastball and the ability to control it has a mighty weapon in his arsenal. Not only is it powerful in its own right, it also makes even a so-so changeup or breaking pitch highly effective. And if you learn how to throw a variety of fastballs—the riser, the sinker, and the cut fastball—no batter will think of you as only a one-pitch hurler.

What the coaches say

DON DRYSDALE If you throw a lot of breaking pitches [as a youngster], you are going to take away from your fastball; it's going to be a yard short. If you become a breaking-ball pitcher, you might not meet your full level.

JIM KAAT [People say] you have to change speeds and get your breaking ball over the plate because all good hitters are fastball hitters. But if you have command of three pitches, you get more people out with the fastball. Even off-speed pitchers; if you check their charts on good days, they throw 70 or 75 percent fastballs.

SANDY KOUFAX Every pitcher's best pitch is his fastball. It's the fastball that makes the other pitches effective. Hitters must look for it and try to adjust for a breaking pitch. While they are looking for the breaking pitch, the fastball is by them before they can adjust.

TOMMY LASORDA The most effective thing you could have [in a fastball] is movement on the ball. In the big leagues, you could stand on the mound with a pistol and shoot bullets at the hitters. Eventually they'd time them. I'd rather see a pitch move half the size of a baseball than see one thrown 95 miles an hour straight as a string.

RAY MILLER Most young pitchers start out with a fastball and a second pitch. They use the fastball to get ahead of the hitter in the count. When they get to a higher baseball echelon, they need to develop other pitches they can throw for strike one. If a pitcher learns to throw something slow for strike one, the hitter automatically becomes defensive.

JOE TORRE There's no question the fastball is the best pitch in baseball. The problem is young pitchers don't throw it enough. They're too anxious to be too cute too soon in their careers. Hitters don't murder good fastballs—they murder bad fastballs.

What the players say

PAUL ASSENMACHER As a kid growing up I never had a good fastball so I started throwing curves about seventh grade. But other fellows my age who threw curves, by the time they got to high school, they couldn't pitch any more. I was lucky! Wait until your arm develops.

JIM PALMER The toughest pitch to hit is a good fastball. You can make a mistake with it and the batter will still pop it up.

Kids who learn to throw breaking balls at an early age often don't give their fastballs time to develop when they're young. They're in a hurry to reach the majors and they think breaking balls will get them there.

NOLAN RYAN [I learned a lesson about overthrowing one day when] I got a two-strike count on Reggie Jackson. I wanted to get him on three straight fastballs. I threw my third pitch as hard as I had ever thrown a ball in my life. I wanted to blow it by him, but instead I blew out my arm. There was no pain in my arm but it felt like a rubber band expanding. I strained my elbow and missed three weeks.

Paul Assenmacher was lucky—he threw curveballs in the seventh grade, but did not suffer any arm damage. He strongly recommends staying away from breaking pitches until your arm develops.

It takes a lot of throwing to develop arm strength and a good fastball. That's why Jim Palmer suggests you concentrate your efforts on improving your fastball instead of working on breaking pitches.

Changeup

The typical changeup, also known as a change-of-speeds, looks like a fastball but reaches the plate at a much slower speed. A pitcher with a good changeup uses the same motion, hand position, arm speed, and delivery as he does on the fastball. Because the objective is to reduce the velocity of the pitch, however, for this pitch, unlike the fastball, the pitcher leads with his elbow rather than his wrist. The result is that the pitch, thrown entirely with the force of the forearm, travels more slowly than the fastball even though the arm speed is the same. Also, and this is critical, changeup grips are not the same as fastball grips.

One way of gripping the ball for a changeup is to push it deep into the palm and place the thumb on the side of the ball rather than underneath it. The decrease in speed comes from the absence of thumb pressure to boost the backward rotation of the fastball. Another changeup grip—the more conventional one in decades past—is to spread three fingers slightly apart and grip the ball across the horizontally held seams; here the speed is dissipated by the drag of the third finger.

Either method results in a pitch with looser rotation and thus less speed; in fact, the changeup grip slows the fastball down by 15 to 20 percent. Anything slower gives the batter time to adjust, while anything faster becomes little more than a mediocre fastball. The essential ingredient of a changeup that works is the differential in speed between it and the fastball you would like the batter to think it is.

A changeup off the four-seam fastball is known as a "straight change," for reasons that are clear. But a changeup can also drop or sail if it is thrown with the seams in the position of the sinking fastball.

While the four-seam fastball may travel 92-95 m.p.h., the two-seamer 88-91 m.p.h., and the curveball 78-79 m.p.h., the changeup may approach the plate as slowly as 72-73 m.p.h.—hardly fast enough to warrant a speeding ticket.

A hitter who expects a fastball but receives a

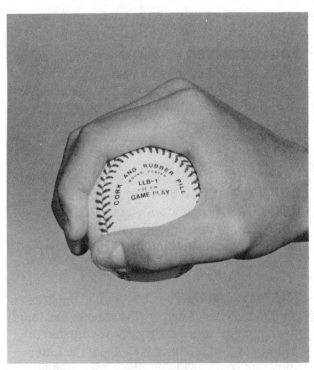

The changeup is thrown exactly the same as a fastball except that the ball is held way back in the palm of the hand with the thumb on the side.

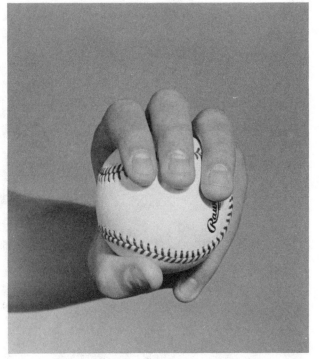

A changeup also can be thrown by spreading three fingers slightly apart while gripping the ball across the horizontally held seams.

changeup rarely hits the ball well. It's that surprising difference in the speed of the ball—when the speed of the arm swing is exactly the same as for the fastball—that throws him off balance, often causing him to swing and miss, or to stand there stunned while the off-speed pitch loops lazily past. That is why the change can be the pitch-of-choice when pitchers fall behind in the count. But for young pitchers, beware: the changeup is a great pitch once you have achieved control of it, but it is notoriously hard to control. It is a tricky thing to throw hard and deliver soft.

If you ease up on your motion, you will tip off the batter that your slowball is coming—you must throw the changeup with exactly the same delivery and motion as the fastball. Controlling the change is a matter of feel—be sensitive to how the ball feels as it leaves your hand when you throw it for a strike, and how it feels when the ball slips out early and flies over the catcher's head.

Several active pitchers practice a relatively new pitch called the circle change. If you join the tips of the thumb and index finger as if you were making the "OK" sign, while holding the ball deep in your palm, you will be forming the "circle change" that has been the key to success for Frank Viola in recent years. Even Nolan Ryan of the Texas Rangers has mastered the pitch, giving him yet another weapon for his fabulous forties. With the circle change, the pitcher uses normal arm speed but slows the ball by using his knuckles rather than fingertips as release pressure points.

In addition to the standard changeup and the circle change, other pitches have also been used to differentiate from the fastball. The palmball, slip pitch, forkball, split-fingered fastball, knuckleball, and even the occasional floater have served the purpose well. More about these pitches in the next chapter.

Mike Boddicker "turned over" his changeup and created what he calls a foshball.

What the coach says

EARL WEAVER If a guy has an 82-m.p.h. fastball, a 78-m.p.h. changeup won't do him any good. But if a guy has a 90-m.p.h. fastball and a 78-m.p.h. change, that will work because there's a big enough difference.

What the pitchers say

MIKE BODDICKER I throw a pitch I call a foshball. It's a fastball with a little slosh thrown in, the turn of the forkball, sort of like a screwball. The pitch is nothing more than a glorified changeup.

TOMMY JOHN The changeup is the greatest pitch in baseball. I just wish someone had taught me to change speeds when I was younger.

The secret of pitching is to make the hitter think you're throwing a little harder than you are or a little slower than you are. When I threw on the side, someone looking at me from the dugout would have thought I had nothing. But when it got up to the plate, the ball came in a little harder and moved a little more.

NOLAN RYAN On nights when I don't have a good curveball, the change keeps hitters from sitting on my fastball. It's helped me pitch more innings and get more strikeouts. When hitters see me for the first time, they go up to the plate thinking they're going to see fastballs. But they don't realize how important the changeup and curveball are to me.

Tommy John believes that the secret of pitching is to make the hitter think you're throwing faster or slower than you really are.

William Arthur "Candy" Cummings, left, with a Star of Brooklyn Base Ball Club team-mate in 1869. His plaque at the National Baseball Hall of Fame credits him with being the father of the modern curveball.

CHAPTER 5

Pitches You Can Throw Later

As we cautioned you in the previous chapter: *do not attempt to throw breaking pitches until you are ready for them*! How will you know when you're ready? We could say when you are 14 or 15 and let it go at that, but many kids this age are definitely *not* ready to throw breaking pitches. In truth there are several answers to the question of readiness: when your coach and/or doctor tell you are; when you can get your fastball and change over the plate reliably; when your physique and your command of sound pitching mechanics permit you to throw hard and often, without strain or soreness; and for some of the more eccentric pitches, when your fingers are long enough to manage the grip.

Because the message is so important, we will repeat the words of the previous chapter: *Throwing curves, screwballs, and sliders at this point in your life poses a very real threat of injury to your arm,* and besides, it keeps you from mastering the fastballs and changeups you need to succeed in various organized youth leagues. Premature reliance upon breaking pitches can also stunt the development of your arm strength, depriving you—perhaps forever—of the velocity you can achieve only by throwing fastballs, fastballs, and more fastballs.

That being said, we acknowledge the fascination that breaking pitches hold for the young pitcher—it does seem magical that one can make a large object like a baseball change flight in mid-air. And the time will come, in your mid-teens, when you will begin to experiment with them. We'll show you the way major leaguers throw breaking balls.

So let's begin our examination of the crooked pitches with the grand-daddy of them all, the curve.

Curveball

In 1864 or so, about a dozen years before the founding of the National League gave birth to major league baseball, the curveball became part of the game.

A teenager named William Arthur Cummings noticed that clam shells he found on the Brooklyn beach curved when he threw them. He applied the same technique to a baseball by using a twist of the wrist and a late release with the fingers.

Though skeptics insisted the pitch was an optical

illusion, Cummings used it to star for a local amateur team before signing with the Brooklyn Excelsiors, an early professional outfit. There he earned the nickname "Candy," which was then used to signify a star. Though some baseball historians champion other pitchers as the true inventor of this wondrous pitch, the bronze plaque for Candy Cummings in Cooperstown salutes him as the father of the modern curveball.

Actually the curveball is itself a father—the originator of a family of breaking pitches that includes the slider, screwball, palmball, knuckleball, forkball, split-fingered fastball, and various assorted relatives.

Any of those breaking balls—or several of them—make a perfect complement to the fastball of an adult pitcher. And all pose dire threats to young,

developing arms. Once again, *we strongly advise you to develop your fastball and changeup, and leave the curveball for later years.*

Frank Viola of the New York Mets was 9 when he was warned of the danger during a 1969 kiddie clinic hosted by Jerry Koosman and Bud Harrelson. He heeded their advice and didn't attempt to throw a breaking ball until he was a junior in high school. Like Viola, Bert Blyleven of the California Angels rode the curve to major league stardom, but he was not allowed to throw it as a youngster because his father had heard Sandy Koufax on the radio warning young pitchers not to throw curves.

When Candy Cummings invented the curve, pitchers were permitted only an underhand delivery. His curve, and those of other early hurlers, had only a lateral movement. Early overhand pitchers also threw a curve that broke only from one side of the plate to the other—the curve that today is referred to disparagingly as a "roundhouse" or "schoolboy" curve because it is so easy for the batter to read. (The National Bureau of Standards found that such pitches may rotate 18 times and curve 17′ inches en route to the plate.) The modern curve can be made to move both sideways *and* down, though the vertical movement is far more difficult for the batter to adjust to than the horizontal. The arc of each curve varies in direct proportion to the size and ability of the pitcher, the stitching of the baseball, prevailing weather conditions, and assorted other factors.

The typical curveball may be ten miles an hour slower than a fastball thrown by the same pitcher. To the batter it appears to break sharply downward when it is ten or twenty feet from him. In fact, the curve of the ball is a constant from the moment it leaves the pitcher's hand, but because of the physical limitations of vision, the batter does not pick up the curvature until the pitch is halfway home.

The curve is the perfect partner for the fastball, if you can control it. By that we mean not only get it over the plate, but also keep it down in the strike zone: a curve ball that descends only to the belt buckle is what is known as a hanging curveball; it is also known, all too often, as an extra-base hit. The

When Frank Viola was 9, he was warned by his future manager, Buddy Harrelson, during a baseball clinic to avoid throwing the curveball. Viola didn't throw the pitch until he was in high school.

curve is not a forgiving pitch in the way that a fastball is.If the batter knows you have a good curve, that knowledge will serve to slow his reaction time to the fastball, making the fastball "faster." And if he readies himself for your heater, he will find himself lunging at the slower, "late"-breaking curveball.

Though some curveball pitchers use the same grip as that used for the sinking fastball, most use a grip with the middle finger extending along the length of the outside seam, not across it. At the moment of release, that finger provides the bulk of the pressure behind the ball while a snap of the wrist makes it spin. The index finger is held close against the middle finger, but off the seam. Both fingers apply pressure along their entire length, not just at the tips as with the fastball. The ball is held farther back in the hand, so that the thumb also applies pressure along its entire length, not just at the tip. The ring finger, which applied no pressure in the fastball grip, here forms the third point of pressure with the thumb and the joined middle and index fingers.

An overhand curve will provide the greatest drop and thus is the most desirable. However, if you throw your other pitchers from a three-quarters delivery, you cannot switch to overhand for your curve; that would let the batter know what was coming. In either delivery, as the pitching arm comes forward for the curveball there is no difference in arm or wrist action from the fastball until the arm passes the ear. As the arm moves past the ear, the middle and index fingers ride up and over the ball, turning (for a righthander) out from right to left. As the ball passes before his face, the pitcher yanks those fingers down sharply; the wrist rotates in such a way that the back of the hand faces the plate, and it is yanked down sharply as well—as if you were pulling down a window shade. The ball spins out above the index finger; it is given an additional thrust forward by the popping up of the thumb. The more pressure applied by the fingers and the firmer the yank of the wrist and forearm, the tighter the rotation and the more explosive the break.

As you will remember, the four-seam fastball rolled off the tips of the index and middle fingers; its rotation was backward, or toward the pitcher. The rotation of the curve ball is downward.

If you yank your fingers too early, the ball will roll off the fingers lazily and break prematurely. If you tilt your wrist too soon, you will achieve a bigger but slower curveball, one that batters love to see. A loose, flexible wrist yields the best curve; the more rotation, the sharper the break and the longer the batter is "locked" into thinking the pitch is a fastball.

If you find yourself consistently throwing your curveball high, the first area to be suspicious about is your stride—you may need to shorten it. Or perhaps you are finishing your delivery "straight up"; the follow through for the curve is somewhat different from that for the fastball in that the arm passes both down and across the body—that is the natural extension of the arm motion made necessary by the yanked fingers and wrist.

Curveball in the dirt? Try lengthening your stride. But the simple answer to the problem may not be

Most pitchers throw curveballs using a grip with the middle finger extending along the length of the outside seam. The ball is held farther back in the hand, so that the thumb also applies pressure along its entire length, not just at the tip.

the correct one: it is best to have your coach analyze your mechanics with you before you start "fixing" what was already correct.

What if your curveball curves but doesn't break? Chances are that while you think you are yanking your fingers and wrist down, as you must to achieve tight rotation and a drop, you are allowing your index and middle fingers to slide *around* the ball, from one side to the other, instead of up and over

---

What the coach says

GEORGE BAMBERGER If a pitcher complains that his curve will never be very good, have him develop a slider. If his curve is coming along, though, have him stick to that before tinkering with a slider.

DON DRYSDALE What made Sandy Koufax so tough was his curveball. His fastball would ride in on you, and all of a sudden he'd start with a curveball. You couldn't look for one and hit the other because there was such an extreme [difference between the two]. I saw guys bang the bat on top of home plate trying to hit it.

What the pitchers say

DOUG DRABEK Don't throw curves. I saw a lot of guys hurt their arms trying to throw curves when I was your age. Of course, it's really up to you, your parents, and your coach. But I would stay away from any pitch that involves twisting your elbow. If you want a pitch other than a fastball, throw a changeup or a sinker.

DWIGHT GOODEN The 3-2 curve is my favorite strikeout pitch. There's nothing more satisfying than that.

NOLAN RYAN My real high strikeout totals come when hitters are looking for the fastball and I'm getting my breaking ball over the plate. Any time you have a high strikeout total, it's because you have a quality breaking ball.

the ball. If your curve has some lateral movement and some "bite" (downward movement) but not enough—the notorious hanging curveball—you have probably yanked down with your fingers and wrist too soon, that is, before your hand has passed in front of your face.

Slider

Though it places more strain on the elbow than the curveball does, the slider is easier to learn. It is a useful tool when the pitcher is behind in the count because the hitter, expecting a fastball and seeing a pitch that spins just like a fastball and is traveling only a few miles per hour slower than a fastball, is likely to be fooled when the ball slides just inches away from the sweet spot on his bat. Because of its deceptiveness, the slider has been enormously popular in the major leagues ever since the 1950s. In fact, Ted Williams believes that the advent of the slider has done more to depress modern big league batting averages than night ball, transcontinental travel, or any other factor.

On the other hand, if the curveball can be described as a rather unforgiving pitch, the slider is even more fraught with peril. If not thrown to the precise locations where it will be effective—low and outside to a same-side batter, on the hands to an opposite-side batter—the slider looks like nothing more than a batting-practice fastball. The movement of the pitch is so subtle that if it is thrown across the letters or over the heart of the plate, the batter can adjust his swing rather easily. The hanging slider ends up, often enough, on the other side of the fence.

Because the pitch does not break as much as a traditional curveball, the slider was once called "the nickel curve," with some derision. The late Charley Dressen once described the pitch as "a fastball with a very small slow break or a curveball with a very small fast break." This is not true of the "hard slider" thrown with such success by Steve Carlton, Ron Guidry, Sparky Lyle, and Dave Stieb, among others, but that pitch—which has all the explosive downward break of an overhand curve plus very nearly the speed of a fastball—places a tremendous strain on the elbow **and should NOT be attempted by any young reader of this book.** A typical slider breaks more across the plate than it does down but, because of its tight rotation and velocity, appears to the batter to have no break at all until it is right on top of him.

The slider is thrown with a curveball grip except for the fact that the index and middle fingers are placed slightly off-center to the outside of the ball. As the ball is released, the fingers give it the sliding motion for which the pitch is named. The crucial difference between the slider and the curve is that while the pitcher yanks both his fingers and his wrist down for the curve, he keeps his wrist locked with the slider.

As his hand passes alongside his ear, his fingers—which for the fastball and the curveball were on top of the ball—are now positioned at an angle. The ball thus rolls out of the hand with an off-center spin. So, while the fastball has backspin and the curveball forward spin, the slider has sidespin. It slides some six inches down and away from the same-side hitter, while its curveball cousin falls more sharply.

The slider is thrown with a curveball grip except for the fact that the index and middle fingers are placed slightly off-center to the outside of the ball.

Thrown from the same three-quarters overhand motion used for the fastball, the slider is easier on the wrist than the curve but often tougher on the elbow; to give the pitch its proper break, slightly down and sideways, it is necessary to keep the elbow up throughout the delivery. Think of passing a football, and you have a good idea of how a slider is thrown—and why it makes young elbows turn to jelly. *Think of throwing a slider only if you are fairly far along in your baseball development and you have been advised that your curveball will never be up to par.*

What the coaches say

RAY MILLER You can adjust to a curve or a changeup because you can see it coming much sooner. Thrown properly, the slider causes hitters to decelerate their swings at the last second. That causes groundballs to short by righthanded hitters or grounders to second by lefty hitters.

WALT MASTERSON The pitch started out in the 1930s as a flat slider, a sailing fastball. Now they throw one that goes down, and that's the devil.

LOU PINIELLA You could ban the curve and enforce the spitball rule or even ban the fastball, but it wouldn't have the same effect on the game as the slider has had. The slider takes an average of 20 points off every hitter's average.

WARREN SPAHN The slider has done more to help the pitcher than anything. It not only makes the batter aware that he's got to look for a pitch difficult to detect, but it gives a righthanded pitcher, for instance, a pitch he can use in tight on a pull-hitting lefthanded batter. Any time you've got the pitches to work in and out on a hitter as well as up and down, you're a lot better off.

What the pitchers say

JIM KAAT I didn't throw a slider until I was 25. The slider, if thrown improperly—and there were a lot of experiments on how to throw it— causes problems.

JIM PALMER The slider is a crutch pitch. It's for a guy who doesn't want to work on a curveball, doesn't want to master a changeup, doesn't want to establish his fastball. Most hitters have a slider-speed bat. That means they'll be late on the fastball, unless they're ahead in the count and looking for it, but they'll be right on the slider.

Screwball

The screwball, thrown with an outward yank of the wrist, is the exact opposite of the curveball. A righthander's screwball breaks down and away from lefthanded batters, while a southpaw's screwball breaks down and away from righthanded batters. Conversely, a screwball thrown to a same-side batter starts out over the plate then tails back into the batter's power, and so is not a popular pitch.

Because throwing the screwball is tough on the shoulder and elbow, learning the pitch is often a last resort for an established performer whose fastball is failing. Young pitchers should avoid it like the plague—because of the physical risks involved, the difficulty of mastering the pitch, and the fact that acquiring screwball expertise requires the pitcher to reverse whatever he knows about the curveball. Too often, confusion reigns.

A screwball is not held like a curveball; it is gripped along the *inside* of the long seams, with the index and middle fingers placed on the opposite side from that used in the traditional curveball grip. The screwball motion begins like the fastball motion but changes when the arm moves past the head. The righthanded pitcher turns his wrist and arm counterclockwise so that the arm moves away from the body rather than in toward it. The follow-through is a contortionist's nightmare, finishing at the body's far right.

At the turn of the century, Christy Mathewson used the pitch, which he called the fadeaway, as a changeup en route to 373 wins and a berth in the Baseball Hall of Fame. The late Roger Bresnahan, who caught Mathewson for the New York Giants, recalled that the pitcher only threw it ten or twelve times a game because he was concerned about the danger of injury to his pitching arm.

"Matty threw it overhand, just like his fastball," Bresnahan explained. The apparent action of the pitch from his vantage point behind the plate may have been contrary to the laws of physics, but you can bet this is how batters saw Matty's fadeaway, too. "He let it go shoulder high, with plenty on it, but just before it reached the plate the ball lost all its zip and just floated down over the plate. He was more effective against lefty hitters than righthanders because the pitch broke away from them."

Carl Hubbell, who also starred with the Giants and found his way to Cooperstown, threw his version of the fadeaway harder and more often—sometimes 100 times in a game. Renamed the screwball by a teammate who called it "the screwiest pitch I ever saw," it twisted Hubbell's pitching arm permanently away from his body, with his palm facing outward, and caused calcium deposits in his pitching elbow.

The screwball is gripped along the inside of the long seams.

Today's most prominent practitioner of the screwball is the Dodgers' Fernando Valenzuela. He has had his share of arm troubles, too, and some have argued that overreliance on the screwball cost him five to seven miles per hour off the fastball he brought to the majors in 1980. Bottom line for young pitchers: *stay away from the screwball.*

Knuckleball

While the screwball takes a considerable toll on the arm of the man who throws it, the knuckleball poses no such hazard. It poses so little strain on the arms of those who throw it that knuckleball pitchers can work often and enjoy unusually long careers.

So why is the knuckler in this chapter, along with other forbidden pitches, rather than in Chapter 4? Because young pitchers who fool around with the butterfly pitch may be tempted to work on it while neglecting the fastball and the development of their arm muscles. And besides, the knuckler is the most unpredictable of pitches; even if you tie the batters into knots, you'll get your catchers so banged up and frustrated they won't even want to look at you. When knuckleball pitchers work, the number of passed balls and wild pitches always increases.

Gripped with the fingernails digging into the seams and the first joint of the thumb along the lower seam, the knuckleball is thrown—or, more accurately, pushed—with an overhand or three-quarters motion that includes a minimal snap of the wrist. The result is a pitch that flutters rather than spins, riding the wind currents on an unpredictable path to the plate. The key to success with the knuckler is to find the speed at which it works best for you. Generally, the harder they are thrown, the less the air is permitted to act on the ball. Try to keep in mind that while you are the one throwing the knuckler, you are not the one making it dance. Try to impose your will on the pitch, and it will come screaming back at you as a line drive.

"Nobody ever masters the knuckleball," said Hoyt Wilhelm, who started throwing it in high school and continued for thirty professional seasons, primarily as a reliever. "I never knew what it was going to do. It never did the same thing twice in a row."

Both Wilhelm, a Hall of Fame member, and fel-

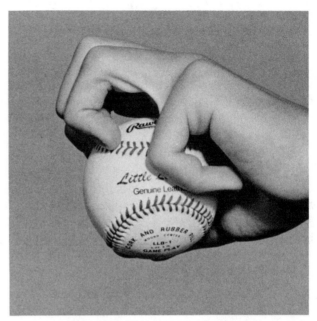

The knuckleball is thrown with the fingernails digging into the seams of the ball.

low knuckleballer Phil Niekro, a Cooperstown candidate, threw the floater by pushing it off their fingers, extending the contracted digits to their fullest at the moment of release. The ball would rotate ever so slowly for Wilhelm or, for Niekro, not at all. The pitch had to be thrown with some precision—not too hard, not too soft—and much prayer. In 1979, for example, Niekro led the National League in games started, wins, losses, complete games, walks, wild pitches, hits allowed, and hit batsmen. (No one charged the mound, however: getting hit with a 70-m.p.h. pitch was more embarrassing than damaging.)

What the pitcher says

HOYT WILHELM: If I was getting it over, I used it 95 to 98 percent of the time. I figured I'd be giving in to the hitter if I went away from it in tight situations. On days when I was getting good movement on the ball, I just lobbed it in. It was just like playing catch. The knuckleball isn't hard on the arm. You don't twist the arm and you don't throw hard.

Palmball

The palmball is an uncommon, unorthodox breaking pitch held deep in the palm and gripped with all five fingers to obtain maximum drag. Thrown with a pushing motion similar to the one used by knuckleball pitchers, the typical palmball rotates little if at all and has a break that is unpredictable.

As if he were a shot-putter, the pitcher keeps his hand behind the ball as he releases it, using the same motion as that for the fastball. The fingertips have nothing to do with the path taken by the pitch, which is used as a changeup to complement a delivery with more velocity. Prominent palmballers are few and far between; two whose names you may recognize are relievers Jim Konstanty, who won the National League's MVP Award in 1950, and Dave Giusti, the Pirates' top fireman in the early 1970s.

Some pitchers throw the slip pitch, a relative to the palmball that was the creation of Baltimore manager Paul Richards and became the trademark pitch of the young "Baby Bird" staff of the 1960s. The ball is not buried in the palm and the hand is rotated slightly outside. Like a watermelon seed that squirts out of your hand, the pitch slips out between the thumb and fingers when released—hence its name.

Forkball

Like the knuckleball, the forkball is a nonspinning trick pitch likely to take an unusual path to home plate. The forkball usually dips sharply downward—though not always.

The pitch is named for its grip: the ball is jammed between two fingers spread apart unnaturally far. Pitchers with long fingers have an easier time mastering it.

Thrown with a fastball motion but less velocity, the forkball is usually employed as a changeup, although it has been the principal pitch for a few very successful hurlers. The forkball requires the pitcher to keep his wrist stiff until the last minute. Just before the ball is released from the "V" of the index and middle fingers, the wrist snaps forward and down. An alternative way of providing the topspin that makes the ball dip is to push with the thumb at the moment of release. The pitch is relatively easy to throw, but because of the need to maintain a stiff wrist it's still not recommended for most beginners, especially Little Leaguers whose hands have not grown to full size. Like the knuckleball, the forkball also presents a problem for inexperienced catchers because you never know what it's going to do.

Relief ace Roy Face made extensive use of the forkball during the late 1950s and '60s, while today Oakland pitcher Dave Stewart is the leading active exponent of the pitch. The traditional forkball is sometimes described as a changeup sinker because pitchers who throw it usually use it to set up other pitches. More recently, however, the forkball has been suffering an identity crisis caused by the widespread use of a derivative pitch, the split-fingered fastball.

Split-Fingered Fastball

The primary difference between the forkball and the split-fingered fastball is that the latter pitch is thrown harder.

While the forkball is an off-speed pitch held with the ball deep in the palm of the hand, the split-fin-

What the coach says

DAVE DUNCAN The forkball is a highly individualistic pitch. Everyone throws it differently, according to the length of his fingers, his hand position, and the way the ball rolls off his fingers. But it's a lot easier to teach than a straight changeup. Hard throwers sometimes take two or three years to learn a changeup and a lot of times it will mess up their delivery.

What the pitcher says

DAVE STEWART I have three or four different ways of using it, so it's like having several pitches. I can change speeds and make it run in or out. You have to throw it hard enough so it doesn't hang and you don't have to worry about your catchers not being able to block it.

gered fastball is thrown with the arm speed and motion of a fastball but a different grip: the fingers are spread as wide as possible but parallel to (rather than across) the seams and the ball is not buried in the palm of the hand. The slower forkball flutters unpredictably to the plate like a knuckleball, but the split-fingered fastball has both velocity and dramatic sinking action.

Because it does not require elbow or wrist twists, the split-fingered fastball is easier on the arm than the curve or slider. Problems are few: finger-numbing cold weather makes the pitch especially tough to control, and finger strains are a possibility (preventative finger exercises are recommended for pitchers who practice the pitch).

Throwing the split-fingered fastball is relatively simple. "You spread your fingers as far apart as you want and throw your fastball," explained former pitcher Roger Craig, who perfected the pitch during the 1978-79 off-season. "It's the same arm action, and it looks like a fastball but then drops."

Craig, a former pitching coach who now manages the San Francisco Giants, developed his split-finger technique while looking for a pitch that youngsters could use without hurting their arms.

"I talked to a lot of orthopedic surgeons and they agreed that one should never teach a Little League pitcher to throw a breaking ball until he's 14, 15, or 16," he remembered. "But even young pitchers need something more than a fastball. I decided to try spreading my fingers in a forkball grip while throwing the fastball. I was absolutely amazed at what 14- and 15-year-olds could make the ball do, and I knew it would work in the major leagues too."

Bruce Sutter used the split-fingered fastball to save 300 games, third on the career list for relievers, while Mike Scott became the top starter of the Houston Astros after learning the pitch. Both have unusually large hands—making it easier to spread their fingers far apart, throw the ball harder, and even "turn it over" (for a curve or screwball type of lateral movement) on occasion.

Like Sutter before him, Scott throws his splitter at 85 m.p.h., 12 m.p.h. faster than the typical forkball but just 1 m.p.h. slower than the average fastball. When a Scott splitter is at its unhittable best, it seems to combine the speed of a Nolan Ryan fastball and the movement of a Ryan curve. "It's like a fastball with a bomb attached," said National League umpire Doug Harvey.

Split-fingers thrown hard break more dramatically. Hitters struck out by the pitch often return to their dugouts complaining that "the bottom dropped out." Though the pitch often winds up outside the strike zone, fastball-oriented hitters can't ignore it.

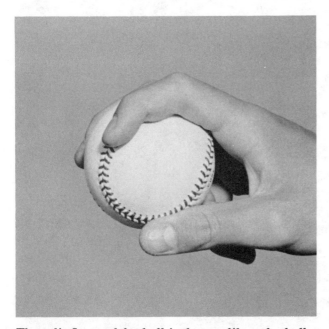

The split-fingered fastball is thrown like a fastball, but is held with the fingers spread as wide as possible and parrellel to the seams.

What the players say

TONY GWYNN If more pitchers had it, there wouldn't be any hitters in the league. There'd just be pitchers and catchers playing catch.

DALE MURPHY It's hard to lay off that pitch. First it looks like a fastball. Then you think it's a changeup. Then it drops.

MIKE SCOTT If the count is 0-2 and there's no one on base, I thow it really hard. It's either going to be a great pitch or a ball.

Reliever Dennis Eckersley of the Oakland Athletics is the game's top control pitcher; in 1989 he walked only 3 men in 58 innings.

CHAPTER 6

Targeting the Strike Zone

Now you know how to throw—the mechanics—and what to throw—the pitches. In the next few chapters you'll learn where and when to throw them, and what other things besides throwing you can do to help your team win. Once you have mastered all these aspects of your chosen craft, you'll be more than a thrower. You will be a pitcher.

The first step, once you have absorbed your grounding in the basics, is to achieve control. Hall of Fame manager Joe McCarthy perhaps said it best: "A pitcher who hasn't control, hasn't anything." Think about it. The speediest fastball and the sharpest curve aren't worth a thing if you can't throw them for strikes, or "convince" the batters to swing at them because they look like strikes. If you've got control, you can win even if you're not overpowering. When you're not constantly worrying about avoiding a base on balls, you can concentrate on mystifying batters.

From Little League to the big leagues, control is the bedrock of pitching success. It consists of throwing well-placed strikes that are not easy to hit, keeping pitches close enough to the strike zone that few batsmen receive bases on balls, and inducing batters to hit groundballs in double play situations or to pop up in sacrifice bunt situations.

There are two basic types of control: strike-zone control and spot control. Just keeping the ball in the strike zone puts the pitcher on even terms with the batter, but even terms are often not enough to get a batter out. Spot control is the ability to pitch to particular spots—low-and-away, up-and-in, or anywhere the pitcher feels is most effective against a particular batter. If you can pitch to spots, you'll be able to direct many pitches off the plate but close enough to it to "expand" the strike zone, not only for the umpire, who may give you the benefit of many close calls, but more importantly for the batter, who must worry about his plate coverage and being called out on strikes.

Strike Zone Control

If you are able to throw strikes without difficulty, you'll be more confident on the mound. To throw strikes you must have good knowledge of the strike zone: an area that hovers over home plate, somewhere between the batter's armpits and the top of his knees. The umpire, the count, the batter's stance, the catcher's behavior, and the reputation of pitcher, catcher, and batter all affect the day-to-day interpretation of the strike zone.

If you observe them closely, you'll note that some umpires are quick to call the first two strikes but more reluctant to call the third. Others call balls or strikes according to where the catcher caught the ball instead of watching the ball's path through the strike zone. The height of the umpire also plays a role in the way he judges pitches. Take note of these factors and pitch accordingly.

Because stars at any level, from youth leagues to the majors, are preceded by their reputations, some umpires subconsciously allow top pitchers wider strike zones, while giving the best hitters smaller zones, though exactly who gets the biggest advantage is the subject of considerable debate. Pitchers and hitters each feel that they are being slighted.

The strike zone can also be distorted by the batter's stance. No one has approached the inch-and-a-half strike zone of Eddie Gaedel, the 3'7" midget who batted for Bill Veeck's St. Louis Browns as a publicity stunt in 1951, but several players have effectively altered the zone with exaggerated stances.

Getting a high strike called against a player like Oakland's Rickey Henderson, who crouches at the plate, is baseball's version of "Mission Impossible."

The umpires themselves admit the human factor does create differences.

"All anybody wants is consistency from an umpire," said Tim McClelland. "When the players know a certain pitch is always going to be a strike, they want to know it from the first pitch of the game to the last pitch, whether it be the first strike or the third. That's what most umpires try to do."

Spot Control

Before he mastered the art of getting his famous fastball through the strike zone, Nolan Ryan managed to lead his league in both strikeouts and walks a record six different times. Tom Seaver, a one-time Ryan teammate, never had that problem. He concentrated on throwing strikes and developed the ability to spot his pitches with pinpoint accuracy. The long-time star righthander of the New York Mets was able to win more than 300 games in his career because of an uncanny ability to work effectively both up-and-in and low-and-away, the two corners of the strike zone that are least friendly for batters.

Low-and-away is a tricky spot that some hitters can't resist and others refuse to go for. If a pitch hits that outside corner, it may be called a strike. An eager batter may be lured into flailing after a pitch that's beyond his reach. A defensive batter, who may be leaning over the plate because he has just taken a low-and-away pitch location for a strike, may also reach outside the strike zone or, more likely, leave himself vulnerable to a pitch that rides up-and-in, but within the strike zone. (Up-and-away is dangerous for a pitcher facing a power hitter because it permits him to extend his arms fully, while low-and-in is often an invitation to disaster when thrown by a righthander to a lefthanded power hitter, who will tend to have a looping, uppercutting swing.)

Before suffering rotator cuff problems early in the 1990 campaign, Orel Hershiser had developed similar skills to Seaver's. Hershiser harnessed his sinker by practicing: throwing as many as twenty in a row to the outside corner of the plate, then switching to the inside corner. His aim was not to throw strikes, but to perfect his ability to throw pitches that *looked like* strikes.

"It was a tough pitch to lay off," said four-time National League batting champion Tony Gwynn. "It started at the knees and went away from there."

Mastery of the quirky split-fingered fastball has done for Mike Scott what spot control of the sinker did for Hershiser. It gave him an advantage over batters by allowing him to get ahead of them.

Cy Young posted a record 511 career victories; they didn't name the award for best pitcher after him for nothing. Although he acquired the nicknamed Cy (for "cyclone") because of his speed, he always said his secret was the ability to place the ball exactly where he wanted it. Statistics don't lie: Young yielded fewer than 2 walks per game over a career that totaled 7,356 innings pitched.

But perhaps the most incredible feat of spot control came when Satchel Paige, at least 42 years old and a long-time star in the old Negro Leagues, tried out for Cleveland Indians manager Lou Boudreau in 1948. The Indians needed him basically as a reliever, they thought at the time, and wondered whether at his age he could still get the ball over the plate reliably. Paige placed a matchbook on home plate, then threw fifty-four matchbook strikes out of fifty-eight pitches!

The Golden Rule of Pitching

Pitchers with control keep hitters in the hole. That is the Golden Rule of pitching. Get the first pitch over. Get the first batter out. Make the batter hit the pitch—the pitch you want, thrown where you want it—rather than try to make him miss it. There are many finer points of pitching strategy, which we will take up later, but the Golden Rule is to stay ahead of the hitter so you don't have to give in to him. The old adage is that a .200 hitter faced with a 2-0 count becomes a .300 hitter, while a .300 hitter fighting off an 0-2 count becomes a .200 hitter.

Pitchers reputed to have good control have a psychological advantage over the hitters even before the first pitch. Because they are constantly around the plate, such pitchers can induce hitters to chase pitches that are off the corners. That is why Jim Palmer suggests that half of all third strikes are out of the strike zone.

When Mitch Williams is on the mound for the Chicago Cubs, many of his pitches miss. But for Williams, whose 36 saves for the 1989 Cubs helped the team win the National League East title, that wildness may be an advantage. The fear factor gives

Orel Hershiser practiced by throwing his sinkerball to the outside corner of the plate. His aim was to throw pitches that looked like strikes.

Mitch Williams uses his occasional bouts of wildness as a psychological advantage over batters.

the hard-throwing southpaw a psychological advantage over batters.

Though he can survive for an inning or two with occasional bouts of wildness, Williams might not cut it as a starter. For most starters, control without the extra stuff is better than the extra stuff without control. He also might not be suitable as a reliever on a particularly weak-hitting team.

Pitchers who work behind in the count often suffer early exits. With ball-and-strike counts in their favor (0-1, 0-2, 1-2), pitchers can throw their pitches of choice. An 0-2 is often a "waste" pitch—a pitch far outside the strike zone that is setting up a following pitch.

There's no such luxury when pitchers fall behind in the count (2-0, 2-1, 3-0, 3-1). Forced to zero in on the strike zone, pitchers often throw pitches batters prefer. In baseball lingo, hitters in such situations are "sitting on the fastball" like lions waiting for unsuspecting prey.

Common Control Problems

Poor control usually stems from poor mechanics, the fear of giving up big hits, or both. For many pitchers, control is like a rabbit in a magician's hat: now you see it, now you don't. It may pull a vanishing act between one outing and the next, from one inning to the next, or even one batter to the next. It can vanish because a pitcher has become "too cute"—working the corners because he doesn't have confidence in his stuff. It can vanish because he has such pride in his stuff that he is always trying to "air it out" to impress bystanders. It can vanish after he has intentionally "pitched around" a dangerous hitter and then can't relocate the strike zone for the rest of the batting order. In short, control can disappear for a vast array of reasons, and be devilishly hard to lure back.

If you experience sudden lack of control, don't panic. The answer is likely to be entirely mechanical and quite obvious to your coach or parents. If the pitches that you once threw for strikes are now coming in too high or too low, the first culprit to examine is your stride. If your pitches are unpredictably sailing outside or tailing inside, check out your position on the rubber. We hesitate to offer remedies more specific than that because we could be "fixing" what was perfectly fine and leaving unattended the true cause of the problem; have an expert look at you. As we said earlier of other pitching problems, when a pitcher gets into trouble with his control it is not because he has lost the knack, but because he has changed some part of his accustomed motion. Almost always the problem goes back to fundamentals. Consult Chapter 3, the one on basic mechanics. When your control mysteriously disappears, get back to those basics and very soon the bunny will hop back into the hat.

What the coaches say

DON DRYSDALE If pitchers threw the ball exactly where they wanted to every time, hitters wouldn't hit .300 or even .250. Pitchers must use the entire plate to be successful.

BILL FISCHER The first pitch is the key. The pitch should show your best stuff. If you could get everyone to hit the first pitch, you'd get twenty-seven outs.

AL JACKSON The modern hitter has been trained to go to the opposite field when the pitch is away. He stakes a claim on the outside corner and he'll lean that way so he can reach that pitch—unless the pitcher throws inside to move him back.

RAY MILLER Getting that first strike is 90 percent of the game. If you throw strike one, you've got five possible pitches left for your next two strikes.

WARREN SPAHN The secret of successful pitching is to be able to throw strikes—but to try not to whenever possible. The plate is 17 inches wide, but I always figured the middle 12 belonged to the hitter. The two-and-a-half inches on the inside and outside were mine.

What the players say

JEFF BALLARD Location is the biggest thing in pitching. A fastball in or curveball away are just as effective as a 95-m.p.h. fastball. Maybe it's my academic background—I believe there are certain areas of the strike zone that are hard for batters to hit in.

Even Nolan Ryan has days when his fastball is around the middle and he can get into trouble. You have to mix things up, give the hitter something he's not looking for. That's my game. I'll always allow more hits than strikeouts but that's because I'm a zone pitcher. Even when I'm 0-2 or 1-2 on a hitter, I'm not necessarily going to try to throw a fastball for a strikeout.

BOB BOONE The strike zone varies far more from umpire to umpire than it does from year to year. You have to learn the umpire's zone—and then, within any game, maintain it or expand it.

OREL HERSHISER Never walk the leadoff batter. He'll score about 80 percent of the time. Even a good pitcher gives up an average of about a hit an inning. You give a guy a free pass, they advance him a base with an out, and what happened to that hit-per-inning? When it comes, you're going to give up a run.

MIKE SCOTT I don't always throw the split-finger to create the illusion it's a strike. I'll throw it high in the strike zone, especially early in the count. When I get to two strikes on a hitter, I like to throw it lower in the zone. That's when it may look like the bottom is dropping out.

In 1990 Bobby Witt finally overcame his chronic control problems and won twelve consecutive games.

Mike Scott likes to throw his split-fingered fastball when he has an 0-2 count on a batter.

TOM SEAVER To me pitching meant throwing strikes—and throwing strikes down low. To be able to throw a fastball on the inside part of the plate, within a realm of two or three inches, is big league control.

The outside corner at the back of the plate was a no-no. To reach it, the ball had to pass through the heart of the plate. I concentrated on the other three corners—where the batter can't get his best shot at the ball.

MITCH WILLIAMS I don't know exactly where every pitch is going. If you told me tomorrow I could have pinpoint accuracy with every pitch, I wouldn't want it.

CHAPTER 7

Strategy: You've Got to Think Out There

Learning what to throw is vital, but learning when to throw it is just as important. Even if you've got the velocity, the proper movement, and perfect spot control, you cannot win without a specific plan for the game and a sense of what you want to throw to each batter, given the situation of the game at the time you're facing him: the score, the inning, the number of men on base, the number of outs, and your history of how you have pitched to him in the past.

The Game Plan

For established pitchers, formulating the game plan is much like programming a computer. Many factors must be considered. When planning your game, you've got to consider your strong points and weak points, the strengths and weaknesses of rival hitters, the umpire's strike zone, ballpark characteristics, and changing wind and weather conditions.

During the game you must be flexible enough to change your strategy as the game changes. You should pitch differently as the score and base/out situations change. For example, you may be reluctant to give up a walk early in the game and risk yielding the game's first run, but you may find a walk a necessary evil later, when you have to pitch around a difficult hitter. And you may again become extremely wary of the walk later in that same game if your team stakes you to a big lead—then you'll want to make your opponents hit their way on base.

Experience against individual hitters is extremely important—but it is also important to follow trends. A usually productive hitter in a serious slump may not be as immediately threatening as a weak hitter in the midst of a hot streak. Also, be observant of the tiniest details: if the wind has started to blow more vigorously, consider returning to that breaking pitch that wasn't moving for you earlier. And keep alert for sudden signs of change, such as a batter placing his back foot near the chalk at the back of the batter's box, a good sign that he finds breaking balls troublesome—he seems to be angling for a longer look at the pitch.

You should keep your hitters guessing by changing your pitch selection and location—unless

John Tudor, a pitcher's pitcher, has thrived for years without overpowering stuff; he frustrates hitters into "retiring themselves."

Ferguson Jenkins contends that it's useful to make hitters think that they have the advantage over the pitcher while waiting for a pitch.

your stuff is so strong that you are overpowering your opponents; in that case, stick with what works—as well as varying the time between pitches. In a tight spot you should usually throw your best pitch—even if it is also the batter's strength. Remember that a game plan forms a useful platform for your mental approach to the first pitch of the game, and maybe even your first pitch to each batter in your first tour through the batting order.

After that, *be flexible, be creative, and don't be too cute*—that is, don't overthink yourself into offering your third-best pitch to get you out of a first-class crunch. And don't let the success or problems that other pitchers may have had with a particular batter weigh too heavily in forming your approach of how to work to him. Other pitchers will not have your style or delivery; a batter may murder their fastball, but that doesn't mean he can handle yours. Re-

member that advance reports and "secret" tips by other pitchers or coaches are useful to establish tendencies, but they are not guarantees of what will retire a batter once the game has begun.

Confidence and concentration are as important to a batter as they are to a pitcher, and anything you can do as a pitcher to shake the batter's mental approach to his task is all to the good. Warren Spahn put it succinctly: "Hitting is timing. Pitching is upsetting that timing." According to Ferguson Jenkins, who had seven 20-win seasons en route to a career total of 284 victories, the pitcher will benefit from anything that makes a hitter think he has drawn the wrong conclusions. The simple act of stepping off the rubber makes the batter wait—and think. Asking for a new ball, shaking off the catcher's signal, or calling the catcher out for a meeting on the mound all have similar results. With no one on base, double-pumping during the windup can also break the batter's concentration and throw off his timing.

In game situations the best pitching strategy is getting off to a good start. That means keeping the leadoff hitter of each inning off base. If the leadoff man reaches base, the defense is disrupted because the first baseman must hold him on and the second baseman and shortstop must shade toward second to protect against the stolen base or sacrifice.

Keeping the first man off base silences the offense, which is less likely to do damage if a man reaches with one or two outs. It also allows the pitcher to work from the full windup—a distinct psychological edge over pitching from the stretch.

General tips for forming a game plan: Fastballs work best on the man who stands near the front of the box, while breaking balls should be served to the batter who stands in the back. Pitches should be kept away from pull- hitters; the result will be fly balls to center and grounders to short (by a righthanded batter) and second (by a lefthanded batter). Keep the ball in on batters who hit to the opposite field. Outside pitches are also recommended for righthanded batters who bail out (step toward third base).

Outside breaking balls work best against the man who stands far from the plate, while low, inside fastballs often pose problems for the hitter who crowds the plate.

However, the ideal game plan seldom works without some modifications. Much depends on the effectiveness of the pitcher's repertoire on any given day; there will be days when his fastball or breaking pitch doesn't come to play. He must determine which pitches to use and how often to use them— and in a jam he must go with his best pitch, even if it is something the batter also likes. And if you have discovered a weakness in a particular batter, don't exploit it ruthlessly each time he comes to the plate; by game's end he may have figured out a way to adjust and he just might cost you a victory. Save some strategic ploys for the crunch.

Psychology plays a primary role in the strategy of the day. A psychological advantage is often the difference between victory and defeat. A pitcher who has it usually has confidence that is as overpowering as any fastball.

Working to a Batter

Establish the fastball. If you fail to do this—to convince the batter that you will throw it for a strike—the batter will sit on your breaking pitch and you will in be for a waxing. You should try to throw the first pitch for a strike, though it doesn't have to be with the fastball; if you are an older teenager who has achieved some proficiency with a breaking pitch and can start a batter off with that, fine. But only a handful of teenagers can control their breaking pitches well enough to throw them when they are even in the count or behind. So let's presume that you will work the batter in the strike zone and outside it by varying speed, spin, and location, no matter whether your "breaking" pitch is a curve, a sinking fastball, a split-finger pitch, or a cut fastball. Here's a hypothetical sequence of pitches to a batter you're facing for the first time in a game.

Don't be too quick to run through your repertoire of pitches or to alternate up and down and in and out. Say you were able to get your first pitch, a four-seam fastball, over for a strike. Use your second pitch to let the batter tell you what will work. Let's say you decide to make him show you that he can hit your fastball by throwing another one, only this time a pitch riding up out of the strike zone. If he goes "up the ladder" with you, he will certainly be looking for a fastball on the third pitch, when you may be able to dispose of him by going even higher. Even if he takes the third pitch for a ball; he is still at a severe disadvantage. He must continue to look for a fastball, and you should be able to freeze him with a breaking pitch. If you see it break outside the strike zone, then by all means return to the fastball—remember, he has yet to show you he can handle it.

Stepping back, however, let's say the batter failed to bite at that high fastball on the second pitch. What then? You will have to return to the strike zone or risk falling behind in the count. Here you may want to show him a breaking pitch low and away. If he lets it pass and it is off the plate, leaving a count of 2-1 in his favor, he will know you have to come to him with your next pitch, making certain it is a strike. He will be looking fastball, because that is the pitch you threw for a strike. This is an ideal time to change speeds off the fastball and get square in the count. By taking something off the pitch, you have supplied one level of deception—don't complicate things by also going for the perfect location on a corner. Simply keep the changeup down. (Alternately, one could very well reason that in youth league competition, you're only doing the batter a favor by offering a changeup when he hasn't demonstrated that he can hit your fastball.)

So now you're at a 2-2 count. You have had him looking fastball, but you have thrown his timing off with that last changeup. What are your options? Fastball up-and-in would be perfect. Another changeup would be tricky, daring, and wide open to second guessing by your coach. A breaking pitch in a good location would be fine, but can you control it well enough to assure a strike? You want to avoid a 3-2 count if you possibly can.

The best choice here looks to be the fastball, which is probably the pitch that you control best. The batter hasn't shown you that he can handle it, and the psychology of challenging him to hit your best at 2-2 is superior to a standoff at 3-2, when you may have to cut through more of the plate to get a strike.

This little exercise is not meant to be Scripture. As you can see, there are several reasonable choices at each juncture. The point here was to show how the batter's response to one pitch determines how you throw the next.

Pitching to Situations

While the level of experience and expertise required for situational pitching may be beyond pitchers of your age, the subject at least bears mention. You and your batterymate are not just playing a game of catch; there is a ballgame going on. For example:

- With a runner on first (or first and second) and one man out, think about keeping your pitches low in the strike zone to induce a possible groundball double play.
- If there are no outs and the batter is weak or the score tied late in the game—in short, whenever a sacrifice bunt seems in order—keep your fastball up; it's tougher to bunt a high pitch than it is a low one, and tougher to bunt a fastball than a breaking pitch. To "sniff out" a batter's intentions in a spot like this, give him a chance to square around on your first pitch but don't give him anything he can handle: a fastball up and in will be virtually impossible to bunt accurately.
- With a runner on second and no outs, a batter will try to hit a ground ball to the right side of the infield, moving his teammate along to third; from there the runner can score on a fly ball. Think about keeping your pitches inside to a righthanded batter and outside to a lefthanded one.
- If you are presented with a man on third and fewer than two outs, you have to go for strikeout or a weak grounder. To discourage a sacrifice fly, try not to give the batter a pitch that lets him extend his arms belt-high or higher. Work up-and-in and low-and-away.
- If you have a man on first who is a threat to steal, give your catcher a chance by abandoning the changeup and keeping your breaking pitch out of the dirt. Fastballs are the best deterrent to theft, yet you cannot allow the runner to dictate your entire pitching strategy. The most important opponent you have to worry about is the one with the bat in his hand.

By no means have we covered all the possible base/out situations and the pitching adjustments you might consider making. But you get the idea: pitch with your head, not just your arm.

What the coaches say

MIKE MARSHALL The whole secret of pitching is not only having the ability to throw the ball where you want to, but sequencing your pitches properly. It's not location or movement but sequence that's the key. You have to blend the scientific with the intuitive.

TIM McCARVER It's much easier to work a good hitter than a poor hitter. Poor hitters have no idea what you're going to throw to begin with, so why try to outthink them? You go after them with stuff rather than pitch selection.

RAY MILLER My approach teaches pitchers to relax and let the defense do the work for them instead of trying to overpower every batter on every pitch and burning themselves out.

EARL WEAVER I like it when the pitcher moves the defense around. Jim Palmer did it, and it was always because he had something in mind.

Jim might have gone into a game thinking he was going to pitch most hitters outside, so the defense would be set up to play the batters to the opposite field. But as the game went on, Jim might have switched to pitching inside. So he'd move the fielders to fit his revised pitching pattern. That's the sign of a thinking ballplayer.

Some pitchers believe they must make a perfect pitch every time. That isn't true. You can't just lob the ball down the middle, but you don't have to make a great pitch, or the perfect pitch, every time. The key to pitching is throwing the pitch the hitter isn't looking for. If you can do that, it doesn't have to be on the corners.

Neal Heaton of the Pittsburgh Pirates achieved success in 1990 when he stopped trying to make hitters miss the ball and started trying to make them hit it.

Earl Weaver liked his pitchers to move their defense around according to the way they were pitching to batters.

What the pitchers say

FERGUSON JENKINS It takes a smart pitcher to disrupt a hitter's train of thought. To counter a hitter's data, you must feed him false information. Let him think you have lost your confidence, that your control is gone, that you are tired, or that you don't want to pitch to him. Confuse him as much as possible and you'll be way ahead of him.

TOMMY JOHN No other person on the field is required to concentrate as hard as the pitcher. The fielder making a player or the batter about to swing are reacting in a split second, but the pitcher has to focus his mental energies. The hitter comes to the plate four times a game and the fielders touch the ball only a few times. But the pitcher needs to summon his powers of concentration on every pitch.

NOLAN RYAN Whenever you see me with high strikeouts in a game, I've got my breaking ball working. I might strike out five or six guys on fastballs the first time through the lineup. But not later. The curveball's got to be there to set them up. And if you get behind in the count, you can't set anybody up.

CHAPTER 8

Working with Catchers and Coaches

At the big league level, let's say you make thirty-five starts and have your best stuff fifteen times. You might win ten of those games (with no-decisions or tough losses likely in the other five). That leaves twenty starts when the pitching coach and the catcher might make the crucial difference for you between stardom and mediocrity.

Communicating with Your Catcher

The only fielder with a better view of the strike zone than the pitcher is his catcher. Although the pitcher is the most important man on any team, the catcher is a close second. A skilled defensive catcher is a tremendous asset to a team even if he carries a light bat.

On both the amateur and the professional level, the pitcher and catcher work together to keep rival hitters from scoring. Good communication between the pitcher and catcher is critical. The catcher must be able to calm the pitcher in a crisis and demand concentration in a one-sided contest.

Effective signals between catcher and pitcher are important because good hitters will make short work of anything delivered with advance warning. Basic finger signals—such as one finger for a fastball, two for a curve, three for a changeup, and four for a pitchout—can be coded into a pump system to fool potential sign stealers.

With the pump system, the catcher may flash four separate signals, but only one is the actual call—perhaps the third signal in a set. The pump system is often changed during a game.

Signal calling is not always the domain of the catcher. Some experienced pitchers prefer to call their own game and some managers—especially on the amateur level—reserve the right to call pitches from the bench. As a beginning pitcher, you probably will not be calling pitches yourself. If on your team this responsibility is left up to the catcher, make sure that he is made aware of your strengths and weaknesses in advance. Don't go blindly into a game without having worked out an overall strategy for calling pitches.

Even when a catcher does call the pitches, a pitcher has veto power. He may shake off a sign until the catcher puts down one that is more to his liking. If they reach an impasse, a meeting at the mound results. When you are involved in such a conference, don't let your ego get in the way. Listen carefully to what your catcher has to say. Don't back down if you're certain you're right, but remember: your catcher is out there trying to help you help your team.

As you stand there on the mound, remember that the catcher, crouched behind the plate, is observing your every move. He can often notice things that you might not be aware of.

Heed the catcher's advice, both in conferences on the mound and in the dugout while your team is at bat. Your catcher can provide you with advice on fielding bunts, strategies for picking off runners or preventing steals, covering bases, and backing up throws. If the catcher notices that you're starting to do something wrong—dropping your arm, giving away your pitches, failing to follow through in an effective manner, or whatever—he's there to let you

Your catcher can provide you with plenty of good advice, from what pitches to throw to what mechanical things you may be doing wrong.

know about it. More than any other player on the team, the catcher can prevent you from hurting yourself—or your team.

The catcher is also the man on the spot when the coach or manager considers a pitching change. He must be honest when asked whether the pitcher is losing his stuff. Sometimes such honesty can strain pitcher-catcher friendships.

Friendships can also be strained by defensive lapses. Any pitch that gets by the catcher is classified by the official scorer as a passed ball (catcher's error) or a wild pitch (pitcher's error). When the passed ball is the result of crossed signals, the catcher suffers the embarrassment of the error, even though the fault is not his. If he has called for a fastball and he sees it starting out belt-high and inside, he will have to scramble to the other side of the plate if in fact you have tossed him a curve. If, on the hand, he has taken a defensive position for a curve and he gets a fastball, he will probably not have enough time to react, and the ball will rocket past him to the backstop. If you and your catcher are working together effectively as a team, your friendship should manage to survive an occasional crossed communication.

A good defensive catcher can be accused of stealing strikes for his pitchers. He might set up slightly off the plate so that if the pitch does nestle into his mitt without him having to move for it, chances are good that the ump will give him the strike. Or he might receive a pitch narrowly out of the strike zone and snatch it back in, moving only his mitt but not his body. A veteran umpire is less likely to be deceived by this maneuver, but in youth leagues a wily catcher might get his pitcher five extra strikes a game.

Catchers can also provide pitchers with timely advice that means far more than an extra strike or two. A pitcher cannot pitch effectively without confidence, and a catcher can be vital to maintaining that confidence during a game when things start to go wrong, and between outings when the results have been disappointing. The coach must take on part of that burden, too, but sometimes it is easier for a pitcher to heed advice that comes from his batterymate.

Tony Pena of the Boston Red Sox is one of the game's best at stealing strikes for his pitchers.

Advice is nice when it works, but there are many other ways good catchers can help their pitchers: maintaining their concentration, creating high levels of communication, keeping signals hidden from batters and baserunners, spotting potential mechanical flaws, and establishing good relations with the umpire. Catchers who don't dispute umpires' judgment are more likely to get strike calls on borderline pitches.

When a pitcher works with the same catcher game after game, a trust and communication build between the two that is magical. The pitcher thinks about what he is going to throw and where he is going to throw it; simultaneously the catcher signals for that very pitch and location—even if it is an against-the-grain choice, one that no one in the dugout or stands would imagine. When a pitcher and catcher work well together, the pitcher can confidently give over the job of pitch selection and concentrate his mental energies on his body mechanics and the pitches themselves.

No matter what a pitcher throws, his catcher must hold up his end of the battery. No matter what kind of pitcher you are, your success will to a large extent depend upon the ability of the catcher with whom you are paired and the quality of the relationship that exists between you. Good rapport between catcher and pitcher is mandatory—at any level of baseball.

What the coaches say

MOE BERG Pitchers and catchers are mutually helpful. It is encouraging to a pitcher when a catcher calls for the ball he wants to throw and corroborates his judgment.

BILLY MUFFETT What a pitcher and catcher are really doing is playing catch. If they can get the rhythm going and get into a groove, they won't have any trouble.

Bob Boone believes that the most important thing a catcher can do is call the correct pitches.

What the players say

BOB BOONE The catcher is not going to bring any magic—he's there to receive it. If I call the right pitches in the right spots, my team should be successful. The biggest thing a catcher can do is not let his pitcher get hurt by making the wrong pitch selection.

A catcher lives through the pitcher, figuring out combinations of pitches. How does a batter hit? What's he thinking? What's he looking for? How can I defeat him?

FERGUSON JENKINS A smart pitcher will work with his catcher right down the line. Although the pitcher gets the headlines, the catcher is the mainstay of any team. He has to be intelligent, have a good memory, and have an excellent understanding of baseball strategy. The catcher is in charge of calling signals, moving players around, and setting the pace of the game as well as catching the ball.

TOMMY JOHN If you have a good catcher, you go over the game plan of how you want to pitch and then delegate that authority to the man behind the plate. He can see things the pitcher can't. He can watch the batter's feet and see if he is diving after pitches. The catcher can tell me if we've got to come inside more or change speeds more.

A good pitcher and catcher are like a hand in a glove. If it's a nice fit, it's a tough combination to beat.

MIKE SCIOSCIA I think a pitcher has his real good stuff 60 to 70 percent of the time. He is probably going to be a little off on his fastball or some other pitch. That's when we need to make adjustments.

Communicating with Your Coach

If you are a good listener, you can improve your pitching by listening to coaches as well as catchers. While that is undeniably true when you are a young, inexperienced pitcher—especially on the amateur level—it is also true for established veterans in the major leagues.

The major league way to pitch is to gather all possible information, from all possible sources, and apply what you learn to your own natural ability as an individual. Although the stories that follow relate to major league pitchers, there are lessons in them for pitchers at any level.

The benefits of listening to the pitching coach are obvious. For example, tips given to Jeff Ballard by new Baltimore pitching coach Al Jackson during spring training helped turn the so-so southpaw into one of baseball's best pitchers in 1989.

Ballard, knowing the value of a good lesson from his days as a geophysics major at Stanford, immediately practiced what Jackson preached. The pitcher moved his right foot closer to third base so that his fastball would stay in the strike zone more frequently, altered the grip on his fastball, tightened up his slider, and began to throw more curves. Ballard, who had gone 10-20 in his previous major league experience, was 18-8 for the 1989 Orioles.

A year earlier, Chicago Cubs pitching coach Dick Pole had worked similar wonders with Greg Maddux. After the 1987 season, when both men were at Maracaibo in the Venezuelan Winter League, Pole convinced Maddux to keep his fastball down in the strike zone but stop trying to throw it past all comers, to throw his curve and changeup even when behind on the count, and to make some mechanical adjustments on the curve. Over the next two seasons Maddux won 37 games.

Maddux, who has learned it's often better to take something off a pitch than to put something on it, had high praise for Pole. "Dick always reminds me not to get into patterns the hitters can figure out," the righthander said. "That's why he's such a good coach—he keeps me alert." Good pitching coaches not only keep their charges alert but create personalized programs for each individual.

"You can't tell them all the same thing because they're all working with different tools," explained Oakland's Dave Duncan, one of several former catchers serving as big league pitching coaches. "With videotape, each guy can develop a good understanding of his personal basic mechanics and what he has to do with his delivery to be consistent."

Both amateur and professional pitching coaches have to be conscious of the mental as well as the physical aspects of the game. If pitchers don't have confidence in their coaches, no advice will make any difference. A coach who is not a diplomat, who insists upon his way of correcting flaws in mechanics or attitude, will find it hard to get his message across to a youngster. From your perspective as a developing pitcher, with an overbearing coach you may need to muster more maturity than might be expected of one so young—otherwise you win the personality battle by not heeding his advice, but you

In 1989 Jeff Ballard listened to advice from Baltimore pitching coach Al Jackson and became one of the top pitchers in baseball.

lose the war by not progressing in your craft.

A coach also monitors the progress of pitchers during games, and keeps tabs on the number of pitches thrown. (An average workload in the majors is 100-125 pitches; beyond that, a pitcher often starts to labor.) He looks for telltale signs of tiring, such as more time between pitches or fastballs being pulled foul that earlier in the game were being fouled back. He encourages his pitcher with positive thoughts between innings. He also talks to the catcher about the pitcher, knowing that often communication between the batterymates is more effective than that of coach to pitcher.

Regardless of the extent of your natural-born talents, working alone without expert guidance you'll never develop your abilities to their greatest potential. If you work with your catcher and pitching coach, you'll be a far better athlete than if you try to go it alone. Pitching may be a unique part of baseball, but never forget that baseball is a team game.

What the coaches say

LARRY BEARNARTH The big thing is to convince pitchers you are on their side, that you are not correcting them to embarrass them, you are correcting them to improve them.

Larry Bearnarth, the pitching coach of the young Montreal Expos mound staff, knows how fragile the confidence of young pitchers can be.

RAY MILLER You can be more direct with your catcher than with your pitchers. You can tell him which pitchers he may need to be stern with and which ones need a pat on the back. You can even have signs to tell your catcher what he should say when he goes to the mound.

JIM OWENS When I first came up as a pitcher I had a great overhand curve, but they told me I had to throw a slider. So I worked on the slider until I lost my overhand curve. That taught me never to take a young pitcher and force him to come up with a new pitch.

JOHNNY SAIN The learning process should begin as early as possible. I don't mean that a 12- or 13-year-old boy should be sent out to the mound and taught the curveball. But I do think he should be given an understanding of the proper mechanics of all pitches—why rotation is important, how it can be applied, what it does to the ball. Few pitchers can get by with just a fastball. To become a prospect, a pitcher must develop control, a curveball, and a change of pace.

I put myself into the pitcher's place and ask how I would pitch with his ability. I may offer two or three suggestions—he'll pick out the thing that fits, and it then becomes his idea. If you offer him one way and tell him he must do it, he'll build up a wall against it. The man who succeeds is the man who follows his own plan.

CHAPTER 9

The Mental Game

Attitude is as important as ability. Without a winning attitude, even a talented pitcher will not live up to his potential.

A winning attitude has many sides: self-confidence, concentration, dedication, poise on the mound, and the ability to maintain healthy relationships with coaches, teammates, and opponents.

The mental requirements are even tougher for relief pitchers, who are charged with working out of major jams in the late innings of close games. Maybe it's true that top relief pitchers have "ice water in their veins."

Do you want to be a good pitcher? If so, you've got to understand that, like the leading man in a Broadway musical, the pitcher needs to look and act the part. The way he wears his uniform, walks to the mound, or behaves once he's there often reveals much about his confidence or lack of it.

Worried glances to a parent or coach spell guaranteed trouble. So do temper tantrums or angry glares at teammates who make errors, batters who get hits, or coaches whose suggestions are nothing more than constructive criticism. Everyone makes mistakes. How a pitcher reacts to the mistakes of others—and his own—reveals what he really thinks of himself and his abilities.

The pitcher is the center of attention—the man most responsible for his team winning or losing. Because the hopes of his teammates ride on his arm, a pitcher must be mentally and physically ready to perform when he takes the mound. An off-the-field argument with a parent, teacher, or friend could interfere with a player's performance; you're only human, and no one would blame you. But if you're determined to become a real pitcher, you'll have to leave your worries behind once you step onto the playing field. Your teammates are counting on you. Personal problems should not be permitted to interfere with business; the pitcher's business is winning the baseball game at hand.

Because he is usually the best all-around player on his team, the pitcher might have even more importance on a Little League team. But he won't get far without the right attitude. According to Sparky Anderson, manager of the Detroit Tigers, "There's no question about the importance of

Oakland Athletics ace Dave Stewart insists that he does not need his best stuff to get hitters out. Extreme concentration and consistency give him an edge over inexperienced hurlers who rely only on their stuff.

psychology in baseball. In anything you do, if you have a great attitude and a great outlook, you can be knocked to the ground but get right back up to fight again. If you can do that, it will make you great at whatever you do."

Without the capacity to recover from adversity, even the most gifted natural athletes face formidable odds.

"I've seen kid after kid come up to the big leagues with all kinds of talent, but few stick around," said Hall of Famer Bob Feller. "The ones who do aren't necessarily those with the best natural ability but those willing to work hardest with what they've got.

On any level of the sport, the best pitchers always give that extra mile. They have to: change comes suddenly in pitching. One bad pitch in a close game can mean the difference between victory and defeat. Or it can convince the manager to change pitchers.

A lapse in concentration can produce that one bad pitch. The pitcher has to shut out the world around him and direct his full attention to the hitter, the catcher, and the baserunners. Taunts from the opposing bench or comments from the grandstand cannot distract him. A pitcher who keeps cool under fire keeps his control and should survive the occasional rough spots that occur in every game.

Attitude is also influenced by health. Everyone feels better on some days than he does on others. A pitcher may feel unbeatable after warming up—but then he can't get anyone out. On other days, he may be tired or under the weather, but he wins because the other team's line drives are hit directly at the fielders.

"Even when I don't have my good stuff, I can go out and trick people," explained Dave Stewart of the Oakland Athletics. "A lot of guys feel they have to have their best stuff to beat you, but I don't. I feel I can beat you on any given day. I concentrate when I'm out there.

"What matters most to me are consistency, reliability, and winning. As long as I take the ball and keep my team in the game, I'm doing my job."

Have you ever noticed how many of the pitchers with great stuff—Roger Clemens, Dwight Gooden, Nolan Ryan, Dave Stieb—also have great poise? They need it especially, it seems, because they so often have trouble getting loose, putting their team behind by a couple of runs in the opening inning. "Get 'em early or not at all," the other teams know, because while many pitchers have great stuff, these stars also have the mental toughness to weather the storm and win.

For major league star hurlers, keeping their mental composure—or recovering it after a brief lapse—may mean taking their mind off the game situation for a moment and turning it to a quick review of their own pitching mechanics. Tom Seaver was particularly adept at diagnosing and correcting his own mechanical flaws on the spot. You may not be so adept, not yet anyway. Simple relaxation tactics may be just the thing for you—like counting to ten slowly if you sense that your heart is pounding and your mastery is fast, or deliberately altering your breathing pattern between pitches so that you inhale deeply through the nose and exhale between lips that are only narrowly open.

"I don't believe in pressure," said Tommy Lasorda,

Bob Walk of the Pittsburgh Pirates doesn't get flustered when men are on base; he just sets his mind to the task at hand.

Bullpen ace John Franco approaches every hitter as if he were batting .350.

a manager whose teams have often competed in postseason play. "The word is misused. As I travel around the country, all I hear is 'the pressure of this,' 'the pressure of that.' Hogwash!

"Pressure comes from within when you're afraid of failing. I never think about failure. I never think we're going to lose. I create only positive pictures in my mind."

Warren Spahn found a mental edge by setting personal goals, but limited ones. If he didn't win four games per month (20 wins per season), he felt he didn't have a good year. You might consider a more modest goal, such as three innings without issuing a walk, or one inning in which all your pitches were thrown in the sequence and locations you and your catcher had in mind. Even more modestly, but precisely to the point, is to make each pitch exactly the pitch you want. Get a mental picture of where you want the ball to go, and you'll be amazed at how often it will get there. Even a wasted pitch, designed

to set up the next one or two in the sequence, should be thrown with a purpose: make it the best waste pitch you can—don't throw an 0-2 pitch so wide of the plate that no batter would dream of offering at it.

If your attitude is that every pitch counts, every pitch will. Although the pitcher is defined as the linchpin of the defense, you will find yourself thinking *offensively*. The batters, whose job is to create offense, will respond defensively. The game will belong to you. As the pitcher, you are the only one who *acts;* everyone else—batters, fielders, baserunners—*reacts.*

Reliever John Franco's approach to pitching is simple: "I try to visualize every batter as if he's Tony Gwynn hitting .350—even if he's only hitting .250. The .250 guy can hurt you as much as the other guys. When you think that way, you don't have a letdown."

Oakland coach Dave Duncan had this to say of his team's star fireman, Dennis Eckersley: "Eck's makeup explains why he's so great at his role. What he does so well is control his emotions. That's the key—going out and remaining poised in crucial situations. And he never lets the previous day's performance affect him."

A starter should think the same way—even though he only works every fourth or fifth day. Even if he loses, his job is to come back the next day ready to prepare for his next start. He should explore the reason for the loss—especially if the problem is physical—but not let himself dwell on the defeat. Thinking about a bad job the last time out will prevent him from making a fresh start.

Whether a pitcher starts or relieves, he must be fresh physically and mentally any time he takes the mound. A good attitude can convert an average club into a champion, while a bad attitude can sabotage a team of skilled athletes. The pitcher who refuses to lose will instill that same burning desire in the players who share the field with him. They will play harder for him whenever he is on the mound.

That is true even on the major league level. For example, in 1972 the Philadelphia Phillies won only 59 games all year. But lefthander Steve Carlton was so inspiring whenever he took the mound that the

Steve Carlton won an amazing 46 percent of the Phillies games in 1972 when he compiled a 27-10 record and won the Cy Young Award.

Phillies won 27 of their games for him.

"Thinking is the key to winning," said Frank Sullivan, whose eleven-year major league career ended in 1963. "When I pitched, I got rid of all tension. I freed my mind of worry about the team I was pitching against, where I was playing, or how many people were in the stands. I concentrated on doing my job—getting the ball over the plate."

Concentration, coupled with confidence, are cornerstones of the winning attitude. Supported with control and consistency, they can make you a great pitcher.

What the coach says

MEL STOTTLEMYRE A good pitcher needs to have confidence in himself and his teammates. When it comes down to the nitty-gritty, he won't collapse. The pitcher also has to have concentration—to know what's going on in the game at all times and never be unaware of the situation. The pitcher who thinks one or two pitches ahead, or one batter ahead, will always make the right play.

What the pitchers say

MARK DAVIS [on ignoring his recent stats] All I care about is how I'm feeling, how I'm doing my job. Once I start thinking about numbers, I get messed up. I think only about pitches. One pitch. Then the next pitch. Then the next batter.

Every time you walk to the mound, it's a challenge. When the game is on the line, it's even more so. When I get out there, I think I'm the best reliever there is. When the day comes that I step on the mound and don't think I'm the best, it will be time to stop being a short reliever.

DENNIS ECKERSLEY The only thing you can do is go out there not being afraid to fail. My incentive is not to blow it. I'm very aware that it's not a lock. When you throw as many strikes as I do, you're in danger of getting hit. More so in relief, when some hitters don't take as many pitches as they do earlier in the game. There's a lot of glory in this job, but it's terrible when you mess it up.

Mel Stottlemyre believes that a winning pitcher always thinks one or two pitches ahead.

Mark Davis knows not to get out ahead of himself, and to approach each game one pitch at a time.

CHAPTER 10

The Complete Pitcher

You've got your mechanics in order. You have command of your pitches. Your mind is in the game, your concentration locked on the batter and the pitch you are about to deliver. But there is still more you can do to help yourself and your team. The role of the pitcher is unique, and he does occupy the most important position on the team. But he is also a player, with basic responsibilities just like those of his teammates, all of whom are working toward the same goal: victory. If he contributes at the bat, on the basepaths, and in the field, he and his team will have a much better chance of winning.

Hitting

Although baseball tradition excuses pitchers who can't hit, you'll have an enormous advantage over your opponents if you can—particularly if you play in a league which has no designated-hitter rule.

Take the example of Ferguson Jenkins of the Chicago Cubs. In 1971 he batted in the winning run in eight of the twenty-four victories that earned him the National League's Cy Young Award as the league's best pitcher.

"I went to the plate with two thoughts in mind," said Jenkins, who had 20 runs batted in for the year. "One was to make contact and avoid striking out. The other was that I knew that if I hit the ball, there was a reasonable chance it would go through for a hit.

"I put my pitching knowledge to work in the batter's box. I used to think, `If I were the pitcher, what would I throw?' When the ball was pitched, I took a nice, easy, level swing—I didn't try to kill it."

In youth leagues, the pitcher is often the best all-around athlete on the team, takes a regular position when he isn't on the mound, bats strongly, and is penciled into the heart of the batting order. As they progress into higher levels, however, all too often pitchers lose their natural hitting ability because they no longer play every game, and so they don't spend enough time practicing their hitting.

Don't neglect batting practice. If a manager knows that you can put the bat on the ball, that you might get on base or advance the runner, you will stay in a lot of close ballgames and pick up a few extra victories every year.

Even if you're a pitcher who can't hit very well, you should be able to bunt—not for a base hit, necessarily, but to sacrifice your time at bat to help your team build a run. Teams on both the amateur and professional levels often spend many hours teaching the art of bunting to their pitchers. In some leagues, including the National League, pitchers are expected to be their ballclub's best bunters—capable of advancing runners into scoring position upon receiving the bunt signal from the third base coach.

Proper bunting technique may involve switching to a bat with a bigger barrel than usual. The reason is obvious: bats with bigger barrels have more surface area. This book will not go into detail on bunting technique—for that we suggest reading the companion Major League Baseball® instructional, *Hitting*, by Jay Feldman. But here are a few strategic tips.

Because the defensive team usually anticipates a bunt situation, the first baseman and third baseman often charge the plate as the pitch is delivered. With a runner on first, a bunt hit directly at either of them will probably fail; the fielder will throw to second to nab the lead runner. Forcing the opposing pitcher to make the play generally works best.

With a runner on second, the best strategy is to force the third baseman to make the play. Unless the shortstop covers third as the result of a predetermined "rotation play," the third base bag will be unprotected and the runner should be able to advance.

While facing the pitcher directly, righthanded bunters place the right hand on the barrel and the left hand on the handle (the opposite for lefties). The easiest way to deaden the ball is to move the right hand far up the barrel. Any bunt hit too hard will reach the fielder too fast to guarantee the sacrifice.

Baserunning

When a bunt fails—retiring the runner rather than the bunter—or when a pitcher gets a hit, a hit-by-pitch, or a walk, his job changes from batter to

When bunting, your top hands slides down the barrel about a third of the way while your bottom hand remains near the knob. Balance the barrel between your thumb and index finger, but don't wrap your fingers around it—you could be injured.

baserunner. Some pitchers are instinctively good at that assignment. Others have to work at it. If you've been playing baseball for any length of time, you undoubtedly know what kind of baserunner you are. Work with your coach to improve your base running, if you need to. It's a skill that can often come in handy.

Even in leagues that use the designated-hitter rule, pitchers may be inserted as pinch runners on days they're not scheduled to pitch. This is particularly true in extra-inning games. Once on base, the pitcher must watch his third base coach for offensive signals that reveal whether a play is on (hit-and-run, run-and-hit, steal, bunt, etc.). He must also know how to get a safe walking lead, how to avoid rundowns, how to tag up, and how to slide.

A baserunner should lean toward the next base but never stray more than three or four strides from the base he occupies—far enough to get a good jump when the ball is hit but close enough to get back if the pitcher throws over.

The pitcher who finds the bases unfamiliar territory may be more easily confused—and more likely to commit a blunder or be indecisive, suddenly finding himself too far off the bag he has just left and with no chance of safely reaching the next one. He will be caught in a rundown. The object is not to elude the rundown through blinding speed and cleverness—that almost never happens—but to draw as many throws as possible, hoping that someone will make a mistake or that a preceding runner will have adequate time to advance.

The art of tagging up is considerably simpler: a runner on second or third base can advance after a fly ball if he touches the base he occupies. He may not actually leave the base until the ball is caught. Tagging up is not advisable on a short or middle-length fly ball—especially if the outfielder making the catch has a strong throwing arm.

The hardest thing about running the bases is also the most dangerous: executing the proper slide. There are three types of slides—straight, hook, and dive—with the first being the fastest, safest, and most commonly used.

The straight slide begins ten to fifteen feet from the bag, with the bottom leg tucked under the body

Once you release the ball you become a fielder. You must position yourself to field anything hit back through the box.

and the top leg straight out. The hook slide, designed to avoid a fielder with the ball, involves sliding past the base while hooking it with an outstretched arm or leg. Some runners swear by the dive, popularized by Rickey Henderson, but pitchers who use it risk damaging their hands and fingers. Consult with your coach before you attempt to master the dive—considering the position you play, even learning it may not be worth the risk.

If you master the basics of running the bases, you'll not only improve your base running, you'll also be more adept at dealing with the baserunners you face. It pays off overall if you've looked at the game from both sides of the offensive-defensive fence.

Fielding

When you stand out there on the mound, you are not only the pitcher, you are also your team's fifth infielder. You're sometimes the only infielder who can grab a hold of those troublesome up-the-middle scorchers.

The minute the pitcher delivers a pitch to the plate, he must assume that other identity—he must be ready to field the ball, back up a base, or tag a runner. The pitcher must also be able to hold runners on base, execute the pickoff, start the double play, and handle the rundown. He should wear a large glove to knock down balls hit in his direction and to mask his intentions on upcoming pitches.

Except in bunt situations, where the first baseman and third baseman charge toward home with the pitch, the pitcher is closer to the batter than any other fielder. For that reason, he can be expected to get plenty of action—often with only a split second to spare.

A pitcher whose delivery ends with a normal follow-through, which leaves him facing home plate, handles batted balls or bunts like any other infielder—although he should throw from level infield ground rather than the elevated mound whenever possible. A pitcher whose follow-through is exaggerated, however, may have problems.

Mitch Williams, the fireballing lefthanded reliever of the Chicago Cubs, has the most extreme follow-through of any currently active big leaguer. He throws across his body—defying conventional practice—and falls off the mound after each pitch. "I don't fall off on purpose," he explained. "That's just the way I throw. But I probably get an extra five miles an hour on my fastball as a result."

When a ball is hit to the right side of the infield, the pitcher's responsibility is to run toward first base. If the first baseman retrieves the ball, the pitcher will continue on to the bag so it will not be left unguarded.

The pitcher also needs to back up plays coming in from the outfield to third and home. He'll be able to snag balls that get by the third baseman or catcher, preventing runners from advancing on bad throws.

On a passed ball or wild pitch, the pitcher needs to cover home while the catcher retrieves the ball. With a runner on first, the pitcher could serve as a middleman in a relay throw from the catcher to second or third base.

Bunt situations demand analysis and execution. If the pitcher isn't sure whether the opposition is bunting, he can usually find out by taking his stretch, then stepping off the rubber. The hitter—especially if he's a pitcher—often tips his hand.

There are four varieties of bunt plays: the sacrifice bunt, the suicide squeeze, the safety squeeze, and the surprise bunt.

A sacrifice bunt, usually used in the late innings of a close game, moves a runner or runners into scoring position.

On the suicide squeeze, a runner on third breaks with the pitch and the batter attempts to bunt it. If he does, the runner scores; if not, the runner is likely to be out. (This play works only when the

California's Jim Abbott's lack of a right hand has not prevented him from being an excellent fielding pitcher.

batter is righthanded—by standing on the left side of home plate, he'll block the catcher's view of the runner breaking from third.)

When the safety squeeze is on, the runner on third waits for the bunt, then heads for home. While the suicide squeeze is an all-or-nothing play, the safety squeeze is a more cautious approach.

A batter may sometimes try to drop a surprise bunt for a base hit. A slumping slugger may take advantage of an infield playing deep, or a player who can run fast may try to convert a well-placed bunt into an infield single.

In all probable bunt situations, the pitcher's mission is to prevent the batter from laying the bunt down in fair territory. A high, inside pitch usually works best: it will drive the batter off the plate or, if he goes through with the bunt attempt, a pop-up often results. The strategy is different in the case of the suicide squeeze: a pitcher who sees a runner break from third can best get the hitter out of the way by throwing at his shoulder. When he ducks, the catcher should grab the ball and tag the runner.

At any time the pitcher fields the bunt, he should check the infield before throwing. If the ball is bunted hard enough on a sacrifice attempt, the pitcher may have time to wheel and throw to second (or third, if a runner is on second base). If it's bunted hard on the suicide squeeze, there's a chance the pitcher can charge, scoop, and shovel the ball home in time for a play. A pitcher who gets the ball on the safety squeeze can "look the runner back to third" before throwing to first to retire the batter.

The pitcher also has to listen for the commands of his catcher. Since the catcher is the only man on the field who can see everything that happens on the diamond, he'll know how a play is unfolding. If he can't field the ball himself, he'll yell out the name of the man who should and tell him where to throw.

The catcher usually tells the pitcher where to throw on balls hit slowly or balls fumbled by the pitcher in his haste. If the catcher says nothing, the only play is at first base.

Dealing with Baserunners

Another skill pitchers need to work on is holding the runner close to the base and, if he strays too far, picking him off.

When a runner reaches base, the catcher and pitcher work together to keep him close to the bag. Glancing over at the runner from the stretch position will be a deterrent to the runner taking advantage of you. Throws over to first will also serve notice of your watchfulness. You might not want to show the runner your best pickoff move on your first throw over. You certainly don't want to become obsessed with holding the runner close, to the point that your concentration on the batter suffers. And you certainly don't want to be intimidated by the baserunner's antics—bluff starts, jittery movements, and the like—into throwing only fastballs or altering your motion and committing a balk. A catcher who suspects that a runner may have larceny in his heart can call for a pitchout—a high, outside pitch that he can grab while coming up from his crouch and throw speedily, without interference from the batter.

The pickoff play also requires teamwork. Using prearranged infield signals to alert the appropriate fielders, the catcher or pitcher makes a sudden throw to a base in an effort to catch a baserunner off guard.

If the baserunner is too far away to get back but not close enough to be tagged, he may head for the next base—hoping to get there before the ball. The odds are more probable, however, that he'll only find himself in a rundown. When the pitcher has the ball in a rundown situation, his best bet is to run directly at the runner and make him commit himself.

Developing and refining a deceiving pickoff move to first base takes time and effort, but runners will take fewer liberties off first base against a lefthanded pitcher.

Ferguson Jenkins, who threw righthanded, started his pickoff move to every base in the classic way: with his feet straddling the pitching rubber, he took the sign from the catcher, came to the set position, and then gave the runner or runners a quick glance. The throw to first base, the most common pickoff move for a pitcher, required him to look toward the base, receive the go-ahead sign from the first baseman, bring the ball and glove up,

The pickoff play at first base begins when the pitcher checks the runner after receiving his signal from the catcher.

At the set position the pitcher will again check the baserunner as he leads off the base.

Before the pitcher starts to throw home, his lead leg comes toward first base.

Last, the pitcher throws to the first baseman. The pitcher must be careful not to commit a balk when attempting a pickoff.

then make the continuous motion of pushing off with his right (back) foot, planting his left foot, and throwing.

At second, the pickoff is a timed play. As the pitcher comes to the set position, he and the covering infielder start counting. At the count of two, the fielder breaks for the bag. At three, the pitcher steps back, turns, and—if he sees a gap between the fielder and the runner—throws. If the runner has not left such a gap, then the pitcher should not throw through. This option is available to him only at second and third bases; any motion made toward first base must end in a throw to the bag or a balk will be called.

Pickoffs at third are uncommon because the third baseman rarely holds runners close. When there is a play, however, the third baseman calls it and gets back to the bag to cover.

Because the pickoff play requires speed and coordination to guarantee the element of surprise, mistakes are common. They can lead to errors (on wild throws) or balks (illegal moves by a pitcher with at least one runner aboard).

The balk rule, originally created to protect baserunners, contains more than a dozen pitfalls for pitchers that result in each baserunner advancing one base.. A balk is committed when the pitcher:

- While in contact with the rubber, makes a motion to throw home but does not complete the throw.
- While in contact with the rubber, makes a move to throw to first base but fails to complete the throw.
- While in contact with the rubber, fails to step directly toward a base before throwing to that base.
- While in contact with the rubber, throws or

pretends to throw to an unoccupied base, except for the purpose of making a play.
- While in contact with the rubber, accidentally or intentionally drops the ball.
- While giving an intentional base on balls, pitches when the catcher is not in the catcher's box.
- Pretends to throw to any base without possession of the ball (usually while an infielder is trying to entrap a runner with the hidden ball trick).
- Pitches while out of contact with the pitching rubber.
- Works from the stretch position without coming to a full stop in the set position.
- Delivers the ball to the batter when not facing him.
- Makes an illegal pitch.
- Delays the game unnecessarily.
- After coming to a legal pitching position, removes one hand from the ball other than in an actual pitch or in throwing to a base.

Mastery of fundamental defensive skills is so crucial for pitchers and catchers that major league teams have them report for spring training about ten days ahead of the other players. Pitchers spend ample time on infield drills, going over the finer points of covering the bases, fielding bunts, and refining their pickoff moves.

Pitchers like Dave Stewart of the Oakland Athletics, who is one of the best fielders in the game, have a leg up on their rivals before they even take the mound. Those whose skills include hitting, running, or fielding are truly complete pitchers— and so are more likely to win. Teams on all levels are lucky to find them. If you develop such skills, it will give you what may be a crucial edge over your rivals.

What the pitchers say

JOHN DENNY Having a good move is no accident. It takes a lot of work. More than that, you have to do extra work in addition to the usual running and throwing. That's why a lot of pitchers don't have good moves.

As a power pitcher, Tom Seaver had a pronounced leg kick and slow delivery; he compensated for these shortcomings with a fine bat and glove.

I learned a lot about holding guys on from [Hall of Fame outfielder] Lou Brock. He said that runners hate to keep diving back to first base—it makes them tired and defensive.

If you stop the runner from getting a good lead, you take away the possibility of a steal. You make the runner defensive because he is getting worried about getting picked off. If he does try to steal, you give the catcher more time to throw him out.

A good move is like having an extra pitch. It's another weapon you can use to stop the offense.

FERGUSON JENKINS I call the pickoff play Pitcher Magic because it makes baserunners disappear. The threat of the pickoff is just as important as the actual pickoff move. By throwing over to a base once or twice, you remind the runner that you can make a move to pick him off.

WARREN SPAHN I depend on deceiving the runner. The move to first must have coordination. I try to get the movement with my head and my right knee exactly as I do when throwing to the plate. The difference is that, at the last moment, I have to step toward the base instead of the plate.

The runner is looking for the pitcher to tip his move, but I try hard to confuse him. I look at home plate, then to first base a couple of times. If the runner starts looking at my head, I know I've confused him. When I pick somebody off, it's the runner who has tipped himself off.

CHAPTER 11

Conditioning

No matter how talented or physically fit you may be, you need pre- and post-game conditioning. Throughout baseball history all pitchers—beginners and seasoned veterans alike—have needed to stay in shape, between games and between seasons. The best way to do this is to develop a personalized plan and to stick to it. Opinions vary widely about the type of conditioning that works best, however. As a beginning pitcher, you should work with your coach to develop a regimen, or conditioning plan, that's best for you.

Most pitching coaches today are strong advocates of running as a way of staying in shape. Not that running is necessarily a major part of a pitcher's activities in a typical game—it's just a good way of helping you to maintain your stamina. For a pitcher it's a good loosening-up exercise prior to warming up. It elevates your heart rate and energizes you so that you can perform your best. And a pitcher who takes care of his legs will also be taking care of his arm. Many sore arms have been a result of pitchers trying to muscle the ball up the plate in the late innings because their leg strength was fading.

Bob Feller, who broke into the majors in the 1930s, preferred wind sprints to jogging. Jogging—running at a moderate pace for a relatively long distance—is a steady, ongoing sort of activity that undoubtedly helps condition the body in a variety of ways, but veteran pitching experts like Feller feel that wind sprints—running at a rapid pace for a short distance—better condition the body for pitching because they are an intense, concentrated burst of activity that is more like the action of the pitching windup, delivery, and follow-through.

Perhaps jogging is a more appropriate activity during the off-season, when there is more of a need to maintain a general level of healthiness. During the regular season your goal is to maximize your performance from game to game. As the baseball season nears, the focus of your running should gradually shift from jogging to wind sprints of about 100 yards. The amount of running you do should be geared to your individual needs, as determined by you and your coach. Remember that you're not trying to outrun Maury Wills or Rickey Henderson—you're merely attempting to become the best overall pitcher you can, by whatever means that are at your disposal.

Some exercises are designed to strengthen your muscles; others are designed to make them more flexible. Lifting weights is a good way to strengthen your muscles; calisthenics generally help to make them more flexible.

It's good for a pitcher to be strong, but you don't have to be another Hercules or Atlas to be a good pitcher. You've got to strengthen your throwing arm if you want to hurl that fastball at 90 m.p.h. and get the batter out. You've also got to strengthen your hand to maintain a firm grip on the ball so you can make it do the kinds of things you want it to do. You can use weight training to strengthen your muscles, but don't overdo it. Work out with weights about twice a week—never on successive days—and don't try to lift weights heavier than you can handle.

Here is a basic program developed by trainer Tommy Craig for the Toronto Blue Jays that he believes can be used by players at all levels. This is a three-day-per-week program (Monday-Wednesday-Friday or Tuesday-Thursday-Saturday) that works all muscle groups. The amount of weight that can be comfortably handled will vary from individual to individual. It is beyond the scope of this pitching instructional also to be a weight-lifting instructional; consult your coach and/or trainer, or an instructor at your local gym, to help you find the right weight and to show you how to properly perform these exercises.

Days 1 and 3

Leg Press, 3 sets of 10 repetitions
Leg Extension, 3 x 10
Leg Curl, 3 x 10
Calf Raise, 1 x 15
Bench Press, 2 x 12

Flys, 2 x 12
Shoulder Press, 2 x 12
Deltoid Flys, 1 x 12
Rows, 1 x 12
Pulldowns, 1 x 15
Dips, 1 x 15
Triceps Pushdowns, 3 x 10
Push-ups, 2 x 10

Day 2

Leg Press, 1 x 12
Leg Extension, 1 x 12
Leg Curl, 1 x 12
Calf Raise, 1 x 15
Chest Fly, 2 x 10
Shoulder Press, 2 x 10
Deltoid Flys, 2 x 10
Rows, 2 x 10
Pullover, 2 x 10
Bench Dips, 2 x 10
Dips, 1 x 10

You should focus on exercising one muscle group at a time, alternating weight lifting with calisthenics involving the same muscles. You can expect to get a little sore from such moderate exercising. As long as the pain is moderate, you can generally continue, but if the pain is severe or if you feel the pain increase with each repetition, stop immediately. You don't have a quota of repetitions to fulfill. Sure, your exercise routine should be strenuous—if it's a piece of cake, you won't gain any benefit; just take care that it is designed to enhance your performance as a pitcher, not impair it.

One of the first pitchers to lift heavy weights and to advocate plenty of throwing (*not pitching*) on the sidelines to maintain muscle tone in the arm was Mike Marshall, a relief pitcher who also happened to be working on his doctorate in at Michigan State University in kinesiology, the study of the movement of muscle tissue. The pitching fraternity regarded Marshall as something of a nut, even after his conditioning theories appeared to be vindicated by a Cy Young Award performance in 1974, when he pitched in 208 relief innings in 106 games.

One pitcher who was interested in Marshall's

revolutionary notions was Nolan Ryan, who began lifting weights when he was with the California Angels in 1972. Prior to this, weight lifting had been shunned by most baseball coaches and trainers, who felt that it produced muscle-bound strongmen who lacked the agility to perform as baseball players. It has still not gained universal acceptance.

During the season, in addition to his weight work, Ryan does stretches, sit-ups, and step-ups for his legs. He also rides a stationary bicycle and "runs" in a deep-water pool with a snorkel and oxygen mask (water provides twelve times the natural resistance of air).

Ryan's weekly winter regimen now includes at least four days of throwing and three days of weight lifting: squats, bench presses, and military presses.

"I do just enough to maintain my strength," he said. "I also ride a bicycle in my weight room and run a lot—about twenty-five to thirty minutes a day."

Talk to your coach about working out with weights. Nolan Ryan can certainly serve as an inspiration for you, but what is good for him will not necessarily be good for you. As with other kinds of exercise, you will need to set up a detailed plan and stick to it as much as possible.

Whenever you work out with weights, you should begin by warming up with some light running or calisthenics—just enough to start you sweating a little. Then you can go on to lifting smaller weights of three to five pounds. Over the course of a month or so—once you can do the suggested number of repetitions with the the lighter weights—you may want to work your way up to somewhat larger weights. Do not, however, work out with weights larger than ten pounds. *Your aim should be to strengthen the muscles of your shoulder and upper arm so that you will be equally strong across the entire range of motion that you will use in winding up and delivering a ball.* These muscles are collectively known as the rotator cuff, a term that has unfortunately become well known to baseball fans in recent years as the principal area of serious injury to their pitching heroes.

"The primary job of the rotator cuff muscles," explains Tommy Craig, "is to act like the parachute on a dragster. They slow down the arm." As more

Randy Myers, one of the best relief pitchers of the 1990s, chalks up much of his success to lifting weights.

and more pitches are thrown, game after game, season after season, what eventually develops is a cycle of weakness, pain, and loss of range-of-motion in the arm. Then tendonitis (inflammation) sets in, scar tissue forms and eventually the muscles tear. "It's a slow, insidious process," says Craig. But it's not just veterans who are affected. Cincinnati Reds trainer Larry Starr sees Little Leaguers with potential rotator cuff problems. "They abuse their arms," says Starr. "A kid pitches a seven-inning game, throws for an hour later, and then pitches again the next day."

A healthy rotator cuff depends upon proper mechanics and avoiding overwork. But conditioning plays a big part—both in working with weights and in stretching to promote flexibility. On the next page are six exercises devised by the American Sports Medicine Institute specifically for the rotator cuff muscles. If you wish to try them, *consult your doctor first. As stated earlier, Major League Baseball®, the author, editors, and publisher of this book disclaim all responsibility for any injury or illness that may result from employing any conditioning or exercise program described in this book.*

Six Steps to a Healthy Rotator Cuff

The rotator cuff muscles are to baseball—in terms of use and abuse—what the knees are to football. After a regular weight workout, trainer Tommy Craig of the Blue Jays recommends performing a medley of exercises for the rotator cuff muscles of both shoulders.

These were developed by the American Sports Medicine Institute, and are called the "Essential Six." They're performed with five-pound weights for two to five sets of ten to fifteen repetitions for each set.

1. Shoulder Abduction: *Stand with elbow straight and hand rotated outward as far as possible. Raise arm to the side of your body as high as possible. Hold for two seconds and then lower.*

2. Shoulder Abduction with Internal Rotation: *This motion is often compared to pouring water out of a can. Stand with elbow straight and hand rotated inward as far as possible. Raise arm to eye level at 30-degree angle. Hold for two seconds.*

3. Prone Horizontal Abduction: *Lie face down on a table with arm hanging down over the edge. With hand rotated outward as far as possible, raise arm out to the side, parallel to the floor. Hold for two seconds, then lower.*

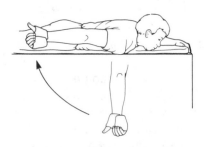

4. Shoulder Extension: *Assume same position, face down on table, arm hanging over the edge, with hand rotated outward. Raise arm straight back, parallel to the table. Hold for two seconds, then lower.*

5. 90 Degree External Rotation: *Lie face down with the forearm extended over the edge of the table at a 90-degree angle and the elbow on the edge of the table. Keeping shoulder and elbow fixed, raise arm to a point parallel to the table. Hold for two seconds, then lower.*

6. Side-Lying External Rotation: *Lie on your side, with your elbow bent at 90 degrees. Keeping elbow fixed, raise arm to a point parallel to the table. Hold two seconds, then lower.*

Though coaches and trainers disagree on the relative merits of running and weight training for pitchers, almost all major league clubs have incorporated stretching, flexibility exercises, and even aerobics into their training regimen. The idea is to stave off the bone spurs and pulled tendons that result from throwing breaking balls, to speed the healing of the tiny blood vessels shattered by fastballs, and to avoid the circulation problems that result from muscle mass.

"Stretching exercises are very important," said Dr. Bob Shupala, former medical consultant to the Cleveland Indians. "You must warm up before getting into any competitive action, whether it be a practice or a game."

While weight lifting strengthens muscles, flexibility exercises improve your muscular coordination. When you play in a baseball game, very few of the actions you will be called upon to perform can be accomplished using an individual muscle acting in isolation. It's not enough to strengthen your muscles, you've got to get them working together as smoothly as possible.

In an article for *Play Ball with Little League*, Gus Hoefling, the Philadelphia Phillies fitness trainer, ticked off nine good stretching exercises.

Don't be discouraged if you have trouble doing them at first. Lots of people can't touch their toes, for example, until they've built up to it. Do the exercises smoothly; never jerk or lurch.

1. **Neck Rolls:** Stand straight with your legs spread slightly. Loosen up. Drop your head toward your chest and rotate your neck to the right. Continue rolling your head in a circular motion ten times. Then roll it to the left ten times.

2. **Shoulder Rotations:** Stand with your feet spread about 6 inches wider than your shoulders. Roll your shoulders downward while bringing your arms up in front of you with the backs of your hands facing each other. Then roll your shoulders up and back while bringing your arms behind you with the palms facing each other. Continue to do it fifteen times.

3. **Waist Twist:** Plant your feet firmly with your knees slightly bent. Twist to the right, bringing your left arm around with your palm facing up. Repeat to the left with your right arm around, palm up. Make it a continuous motion. Repeat twenty times.

4. **Toe Touches:** Stand pigeon-toed. Extend your arms over your head. Bend forward and try to touch your toes while keeping your legs straight. Repeat fifteen times.

5. **Toe Grabs:** Stand with your feet well apart. Turn your body and your feet to the right. Keep your weight on your left leg (slightly bent) while bending to grab your right toes with both hands. Keep your right leg straight. Hold for five seconds. Repeat ten times for each leg.

Toe Grabs

6. **Lower Groin Stretch:** Stand with your legs spread, knees slightly bent. Keep your hands in front. Transfer your weight to your left leg as you squat. Straighten up and switch to your right leg. Repeat ten times.

7. **Hurdle Stretch:** Sit in a hurdle position with your left leg straight out in front, heel pushed forward, and your right leg bent so that your foot is behind you. Touch your left toe with your right hand. Twist and touch your right heel with your left hand. Repeat fifteen times, then switch legs.

8. **Elbow to Knees:** Sit down and spread your legs wide. Lock your hands behind your head. Keep your legs as straight as you can and touch your right knee with your left elbow. Then your left knee with your right elbow. Alternate left and right twenty times.

9. **Sit-Ups:** Lie on your back with your feet together and your arms back over your head. Sit up and try to touch your toes. Hold it for three seconds. Lie down. Repeat twenty times.

Be systematic when doing these exercises. Begin with exercises that involve your head and work your way downward to your feet. Try to do the exercises in the proper manner—it's better to do fewer repetitions of an exercise, but done properly, than a larger number of repetitions improperly. Doing these exercises may leave you feeling a little sore at times, but if you feel any real pain, you've stretched a muscle too far. Be sure to let your coach or trainer know if this happens, since it may necessitate an alteration in your exercise program.

Though the experts agree that conditioning is critical, the exact amount and type of conditioning remains subjective. It will vary according to the needs of each individual player as they are interpreted by the player and by his trainer and coach.

Ferguson Jenkins, the righthander who had six straight twenty-win seasons with the Chicago Cubs from 1967 through 1972, did fifteen to twenty outfield wind sprints on days he wasn't pitching, and

Hurdle Stretch

performed isometric exercises for his wrists, forearms, shoulders, and back. His winter routine included isometrics, sit-ups, and other home exercises, plus three days per week of running and workouts. Basketball often provided an easy way to fulfill the running requirement.

Basketball is not the only other sport that pitchers have imported into their conditioning programs. Steve Carlton of the Philadelphia Phillies advocated not only vigorous weight training but also the strenuous martial art of Sil-Lum kung fu. Mitch Williams, the star lefthanded reliever of the Chicago Cubs, has an absolutely unique way of keeping his arm in shape: bowling. It is unique because no one else at the big league level has done it, but in theory it makes sense: it keeps the arm limber while putting it to a sufficiently strenuous task to ward off atrophy (the natural tendency of muscles at rest to weaken) and adhesions.

Postgame Care

If overuse and abuse are what cause arm trouble, what cures it should be obvious: rest. "I don't care how advanced we get in sports medicine," says Milwaukee Brewers trainer John Adam, "we can't substitute for rest."

Rest is the first word in cure and in postgame care for pitchers. In fact it is the first word in the trainer's classic preventative and healing response to pain—RICE, the acronym for rest, ice, compression, and elevation. The second word, ice, may be nearly as important as rest in keeping young pitchers' arms sound. Many major league pitchers wrap their arm in an ice compress soon after throwing their last pitch of the day: initially to constrict the blood vessels, next to dilate them; the body's natural reaction to cold takes over, and blood flow to the iced area *increases*. The arm is elevated to further ease the flow of blood to the soft tissue of the arm that may be damaged.

Take a tip from the big leaguers: ice down your arm after you pitch. Don't wait until your elbow or shoulder start throbbing with pain.

Mark Langston of the California Angels takes a much more modern approach to conditioning. After each game, the hard-throwing lefthander wraps his

Mark Langston of the California Angels uses a pressurized sleeve to relieve the pain of pitching.

pitching arm in a Wright Linear Pump, an inflatable, pressurized sleeve. The device enables the pitcher to escape the next-day blues even better, we presume, than an iced towel.

Sore Arms

Although proper conditioning reduces the frequency and severity of injuries, pitchers are more likely to get hurt than anyone else on the field. They are not only walking targets for vicious line drives but also candidates for self-destruction. While hard liners can't be anticipated, natural injuries can.

"Man was not made to throw a baseball, serve a tennis ball, pass a football, or hurl a javelin," said Dr. James Parkes, team physician of the New York Mets. "The arm wasn't designed for that. On the major league level, I tell our pitchers, 'When you pick up a ball and throw it, you're cheating right

San Francisco Giants manager and former pitching coach Roger Craig insists that young pitchers never throw any type of breaking ball.

from the first moment. You've got the ability to be really perfect and let your arm get away with it, but you must work hard to condition and protect it.'"

Parkes contends that throwing destroys arm tissue, even in the best player, but that sufficient rest between starts allows most pitchers to recuperate. "Some people have the miraculous ability to abuse themselves and recover," he admitted, "to the vast majority rest is important to pitching. There's no question in my mind that a power pitcher who starts needs a five-day rotation."

Dr. Sidney Gaynor, former team physician of the New York Yankees, agreed with Parkes that pitchers face the potential for injury whenever they throw a ball. "The pitching motion is a peculiar muscular activity," he said. "Every time a man pitches hard, tendon fibers in his shoulder tear apart. It takes about three days for them to repair. That's why, as a rule, pitchers can work only every fourth or fifth day. When a pitcher throws too hard

or awkwardly—if he slips on the mound, for instance—the tear is apt to be bigger, causing a sore arm."

On the amateur level, the cardinal rule of preventing sore arms is prohibiting Little Leaguers from throwing curveballs.

Former pitcher Roger Craig, manager of the San Francisco Giants, is outspoken on that subject.

"Youngsters should not be allowed to throw any type of breaking ball—anything that involves a turn of the wrist that would affect the elbow or shoulder," he said. "The natural way of throwing a baseball is throwing it with your hand on top of the ball.

"In the baseball school I had in San Diego, I used what I call a Little League changeup to give the kids a different type of pitch. It's thrown with a spiral, as if you were throwing a miniature football. It gives the kids an off-speed pitch and makes it easy for them to learn how to throw the curveball when you're ready to teach them."

Little League, Babe Ruth, and Pony League programs have formal regulations to prevent overwork by young arms. Many school programs, however, are more lax, and horror stories about 15-year-olds with blown-out arms are regrettably common. If you feel your coach is placing his team's quest for a title above your long-term well-being, you or your parents will have to—hard as it is—stand up for your right to health.

Dr. Peter LaMotte, former team physician of the New York Mets, strongly recommended that pitchers under age 16 should never pitch more than two innings at a time.

Many medical authorities agree.

"When a young man starts throwing sliders and curves, you're apt to cause a problem that may result in permanent injury," said Dr. Bob Shupala, former medical consultant to the Cleveland Indians. "Growth is occurring, and the attachments of muscles along the growth sites of the bones have not matured."

Rushing tender young arms is never a good idea—not even in the professional ranks. Many trainers and team physicians subscribe to statistician Craig Wright's theory that big league pitchers burdened by heavy workloads at young ages will suffer shortened careers, while those not over-worked before age 25 (while their arms are still developing) often enjoy longevity.

"The average male may stop growing when he's 16 or 17," said Dr. Arthur Pappas, team physician of the Boston Red Sox, "but there's a continued maturation of joint cartilage that goes on beyond that. There's no question that there's a certain connection between the number of pitches thrown and later pitching problems. A young pitcher's tissues are still developing, and he's not throwing with the control that a more mature pitcher has. He can throw his shoulder muscles out of balance."

In both the amateur and professional ranks, the chances of injury increase in direct proportion to the intensity of competition. The increasing use of middle relievers as well as stoppers in the major leagues has spilled down even to the amateur level, where the adage for starting pitchers is "go as hard as you can, as long as you can." There is no letting up, not when victory is on the line and even the skinny kid batting eighth in the lineup can beat you with one well-timed pop of his aluminum bat.

According to Dr. Jobe, "A pitcher feels every pitch is important. There's no coasting period. There's been an overall increase in the level of pitching, and people feel they have to work harder to compete.

"The margin of safety between pitching well enough to get someone out and getting hurt is a narrow one. A pitcher who gets into trouble and reaches back for something extra can produce micro-trauma: ligament strain, elbow or shoulder pains. That's why we see more rotator cuff injuries than we used to."

So be careful out there. It's a cruel world for pitchers. "No pain, no gain" may be the watchwords of weight lifting, but they are, emphatically, *not true of pitching*. According to Dr. Parkes, "Pain is not a sense—it is an interpretation of your brain. What you feel as pain, I may not. People walk on glass or through fire. Some people tolerate things others can't. The same is true in baseball."

You'll know—better than your coach, better than your teammates—the difference between the pleasant soreness of mild exertion and the searing pain of injured muscle tissue. Don't let anyone pressure you into pitching when your arm is sore. A position player may be able to play through pain—a stretched hamstring, a sore wrist—and function at a high enough level to still have value to his team while not preventing his body from healing. Pitching places highly complex demands on the healthiest arm—it is an unnatural motion—and once you alter your delivery to compensate for or minimize pain, your chances of advancement may be shot.

Take care of yourself.

What the coaches say

RAY MILLER Everybody's looking for the easy way out [with weight training]. You can't find a big strong kid who wants to throw year-round, who will stand out in the yard and throw rocks and knock cans down, making himself bigger and stronger and throwing better. Baseball's a basic game. You need to run, throw, or swing the bat. The more you do it, the better you get.

Guys come in and throw hard for a year or two, then bulk up, pull muscles, and become finesse pitchers. The suppleness of the body is what allows a pitcher to throw a baseball at great speed.

TOM HOUSE Right now I'm thought of as Weird Science. [As pitching coach of the Texas Rangers he used hypnotherapy, biokinetics, relaxation techniques, and nutritional guidance; he also has his pitchers throw footballs.] A football is heavier than a baseball so there's some overloading or weight training involved. For it to spiral, it must be thrown with the same precise body movement needed to throw a baseball properly.

What the pitcher says

FERGUSON JENKINS Chop as much wood as possible. The action involved in wood chopping is quite similar to the pitching follow-through. Chopping wood also helps to strengthen back and shoulder muscles.

BIBLIOGRAPHY

The Art of Pitching, Tom Seaver with Lee Lowenfish, Hearst Books, New York, 1984.

Baseball by the Rules: Pine Tar, Spitballs, and Midgets, Glenn Waggoner, Kathleen Moloney, and Hugh Howard, Prentice Hall Press, New York, 1990.

Baseball Play the Winning Way, Jerry Kindall, Sports Illustrated Winner's Circle, New York, 1990.

The Crooked Pitch: The Curveball in American Baseball History, Martin Quigley, Algonquin Books, Chapel Hill, N.C., 1984.

The Game According to Syd, Syd Thrift and Barry Shapiro, Simon & Schuster, New York, 1990.

The Greatest Pitchers of All Time, Donald Honig, Crown, New York, 1988.

How to Play Baseball: A Manual for Boys, John J. McGraw, Harper & Bros., New York, 1914.

How to Play Big League Baseball, ed. Malcolm Child, Harcourt Brace & Co., New York, 1951.

Knuckler: The Phil Niekro Story, by Wilfird Binette, Hallux Books, Atlanta, 1970.

Little Big Leaguers: Amazing Boyhood Stories of Today's Baseball Stars, Bruce Nash and Allan Zullo, Simon & Schuster, 1990.

Major League Baseball Manual, prepared and used by the Milwaukee Brewers, Doubleday, Garden City, N.Y., 1982.

The Pitcher, John Thorn and John Holway, Prentice Hall Press, New York, 1987.

Pitching: The Basic Fundamentals and Mechanics of Successful Pitching, Bob Shaw, Viking, New York, 1972.

Sports Illustrated Pitching, (rev. ed.) Pat Jordan, Harper & Row, 1985.

Throwing Heat, Nolan Ryan and Harvey Frommer, Doubleday, New York, 1988.

Warming Up for Little League Baseball, Morris A. Shirts, Pocket Books, New York, 1977.

PHOTO CREDITS

Courtesy of Boston Red Sox: p. 30, 57.

Courtesy California Angels: p. 81.

Courtesy of the Chicago Cubs: p. 28 (left), 45 (right).

Courtesy Detroit Tigers: p. 2.

Courtesy Houston Astros: p. 47 (right).

Permission Granted by the Kansas City Royals: p. 58, 66 (right).

Courtesy Montreal Expos: p. 60.

National Baseball Library: p. 7, 31, 50 (right), 53 (left), 65, 74.

New York Daily News Photo: p. 8.

Courtesy New York Mets: p. 3, 24, 34, 64, 66.

Courtesy Oakland Athletics: p. 42, 62.

Courtesy Pittsburgh Pirates: p. 21, 53 (right), 63.

Mark Rucker: p. 32.

Courtesy San Francisco Giants: p. 82.

Courtesy Texas Rangers: p. 6.

Courtesy Toronto Blue Jays: p. 22.

TV Sports Mailbag: p. 4, 13, 17, 28 (right), 45 (left), 47 (left), 50 (left), 59, 70, 77.

Cover photo by Tom DiPace.

All other photos by Mike Saporito.

ABOUT THE AUTHOR

Dan Schlossberg of Fair Lawn, N.J., is the only American journalist who writes exclusively about baseball and travel. The former Associated Press newsman has authored nine previous baseball books, including *The Baseball Catalog*, *The Baseball Book of Why*, *The Baseball IQ Challenge*, and the Baseball Stars series.

He is baseball editor of *The Encyclopedia Americana Yearbook*; contributing editor of *Baseball Illustrated* magazine; National League beat writer for *Fantasy Baseball*; and travel correspondent for *Motor Club News*, the official publication of the Motor Club of America.

Dan Schlossberg's byline has appeared in *Baseball Digest*, *Grand Slam Baseball Magazine*, *Peterson's Pro Baseball Yearbook*, *The Sporting News*, *Street & Smith's Official Baseball Yearbook*, *Vista/USA*, the *Official World Series Program*, and many newspapers, magazines, and baseball team publications.

He is the father of Samantha Schlossberg, a student at Glassboro (N.J.) State College.